Praise for *Meet Me in the Strange*

2019 IPPY AWARD SILVER MEDALIST

"Watts renders this strange world, this exotic, futuristic, dangerous world, brilliantly. You can feel the power of the glister rock, the music that surges through the story, through the bodies and lives of Davi and Anna Z, transforming the pair and compelling them to take the biggest risk of their young lives."

—STEVE SHERRILL, author of *The Minotaur Takes a Cigarette Break*

"In an intoxicating swirl of futuristic imagery and existential inner reflection, *Meet Me in the Strange* treats music and spirituality as one and the same . . . a wondrous, alien tale, not quite like any other story out there."

—Linda Hepworth, FOREWORD REVIEWS *(starred review)*

"Drawn with intricacy and vitality . . . Watts successfully captures not only the gravity of a teenage subculture, but also the more mercurial feeling of an axial generation on the cusp of something completely new. A bighearted and imaginative tale about a glam god's fans."

—KIRKUS REVIEWS

"A beautifully written coming-of-age story about all the ways in which you feel most at home when you find the people who are looking for the same home you are."

—Colleen Mondor, LOCUS MAGAZINE

"A fascinating book that blends music and mysticism to create an atmosphere both foreboding and full of possibilities all at once . . . impossible to put down."

—PORTLAND BOOK REVIEW *(4 stars)*

ALSO BY LEANDER WATTS

Beautiful City of the Dead
Ten Thousand Charms
Wild Ride to Heaven
Stonecutter

MEET ME IN THE
STRANGE
LEANDER WATTS

a novel

Meerkat Press
Atlanta

ISBN-13 978-1-946154-15-6 (Hardcover)
ISBN-13 978-1-946154-07-1 (Paperback)
ISBN-13 978-1-946154-06-4 (eBook)

Library of Congress Control Number: 2018930069

Cover design by Keith Rosson
Book design by Tricia Reeks

Printed in the United States of America

Published in the United States of America by
Meerkat Press, LLC, Atlanta, Georgia
www.meerkatpress.com

ONE

It was like she'd lost everything. Her name, her voice, any idea who she was or what she looked like, who the people were around her. The only thing that mattered was right there in front of her on the stage.

We were up close—masses of glam-girls and glister-boys all reaching out at the air like we could feel the music in our hands and pull it into ourselves. Wild kids pushing and pulsing with the music. Not really dancing. But it was music and bodies, so what else could you call it?

And it was the most amazing thing I'd ever seen because the girl was *gone*—not just freaked or blissed-out. She'd let go, totally, of everything.

I got that first glimpse of her about halfway through the show, and it was like I was split right down the middle of my skull. One half was still there with the rest of the crowd, the band like the Horses of Apollo carrying me upward with the fiery sound. And one half of me was zapped by seeing this girl, like a knife juiced with electricity cutting into my brain. She was gone, vanished, disappeared inside herself.

I was cranked up like all the other five thousand fan-kids

who'd come to hear Django Conn, and see him and *feel* him. Some of them had dyed orange, cockatoo haircuts just like Django. Some—boys and girls—had eye makeup, silvery mascara, and big, shiny slashes of lipstick, dangly earrings and platform shoes, feathers and fishnets, and the whole glam look. But this girl was different.

She had glasses, ordinary eyeglasses. They were steamed over and caught the spotlights from the stage, oozy reds and liquid purples. Her hair was black, long and damp in snaky-sexy locks that clung to her face and her neck. And just for a second, I thought she looked like somebody who was shipwrecked, drowning in a sea, dying almost but okay with that, or more than okay, letting the waves sweep her up and away.

I don't remember what she had on. Doesn't matter. Was she pretty? Maybe. Beautiful? Doubtful. Amazing? Absolutely.

She wasn't one of them, not exactly, trying to look like, trying to *be* Django. And neither was I, even though I'd been waiting months for this show, and I loved *Man in the Moon in the Man* more than just about anything in the world. I'd been listening to the new album nonstop for weeks, my new diamond needle wearing out the grooves.

For the song "She's the Hype," the lights went into a wild black and white strobe. Off and on and off and on, pulsing, slamming, stuttering. And the girl kept appearing and disappearing. Not like a ghost all wispy and see-through. In flashes, for a second or two, she was solid, real, realer than anything. It was like the light itself was a drum, pounding light hitting the crowd in sudden bursts. I got a glimpse, and then she was gone. Then back again, broken up into frames like an old film, flickering in and out of reality.

Nobody was paying attention to other people. Nobody but me. All eyes were on Django, and all ears were blasted by the band. So when the girl *lost it*, when she totally lost it, I was the only one who saw and *got it*. Private, secret, just me and her alone, even though we were surrounded by five thousand others at the Maxima. Just me and her in that secret place.

The band got hotter, and the crowd got wilder. Django got fiercer, jumping into "I Asked for Water but She Gave me Gasoline." And I lost sight of the girl, like the tidal waves pushed us apart, a couple of pieces of broken driftwood in a blackwater storm.

Django did all my faves: "I Fear No Venom," "Girls Will Be Boys," "Empire of Light," "Pavlov's Daughters." They finished up with "Flash Bang Baby." And then Django vanished in a sudden cloud, like a puff ball when it bursts and shoots that cloud of dust-spores into the air. It was like he blew up right there in front of five thousand fans. One second he was singing the last line from the last song on *Man in the Moon in the Man*, over and over again: "You're all I've ever had!" Then the band crashed to the end of the song, and it looked as if he'd exploded. It was just a stage trick of course, lights and smoke like a magician uses to cover up his best illusion. But Django blew up and the dust spores whooshed out over us, a cloud of powder pink and velvety violet, and that was the end of the show.

TWO

Everybody hung around as the lights came up. Music got piped in through the P.A. system—a Vivaldi concerto played on a Moog. And it was like waking up from the best dream I'd ever had. I looked for the girl. I wasn't even sure anymore if she'd been real, because how much had I really seen of her? She was just a blur, one girl as the strobe light hit her then a crash of blackness, then maybe another girl, a cloudy flash of faces that blended into one, making that look of pure surrender. When there are five thousand kids and most of them are dressed in glam Django-drag, how could I be sure who was who and what was what?

I stood there, woozy and weak-kneed. Sweet, pearly-blue smoke swirled overhead, like spirits trying to escape back to heaven. Thousands of bodies surrounded me. And voices too: laughter, blurry moans, strained whispers, brain-warped babbling. There was movement in the crowd, but no one wanted to leave. Not yet. We all wanted to soak in the last of Django's shimmery vibe.

It was useless, but still I looked around for the girl. What would I say if I found her? Maybe something stupido like, "Great show. He's the best." Or would I dive right in and ask her what she'd been feeling, what was really going on inside her? She'd been lost. Totally lost and—I know this is the part that doesn't make sense—found too. Saved by the sound. Only how can you be empty and filled up to overflowing at the same time? Possessed maybe, giving up everything then filled back up because the music was so huge, and Django Conn had been right there in front of us.

I didn't move, at first, and I didn't say a word. I'd gone to the Maxima alone, and I'd go back home alone too. So I held onto the moment. For a little while longer, with Django's voice still echoing inside my skull, I scanned the crowd.

It was obvious now that lots of kids were buzzed on fly-spell. I think some of them had been hitting the white gong too—bleary-eyed, tongue-tied, and wobbly on their feet.

A boy bumped into me, giggling and chattering. He had about a dozen rhinestone chokers around his neck and fingernails painted with flames. "I love him!" he said to me, and nobody, and everybody. "Best show of the tour. I saw him last week, twice. This was better than the best." He grabbed my arm and kept on talking. "Django is god! I love-love-love him!"

He realized suddenly that he didn't know me and spun around, looking for the friends he'd come to the show with.

Others were saying the same thing. Nothing could beat what we'd just seen and heard. Django had been on tour for a month with the Reptiles, so the band was at their peak, absolutely together and into it. That night Django went further, deeper, higher than he'd ever gone before. He'd never been so *beyond*.

THREE

My ears were ringing, and my feet hurt from standing so long. The skin on my knuckles was rubbed raw, and it felt like the bones of my skull were still vibrating. And that *feel* kept on going all the way home, on my moonless walk along the canals, back to the Angelus.

The city at that hour was closed up tight: shuttered, locked, and dark as the cathedral crypts. Another night, I might've enjoyed being out alone, sneaking through the shadows. But my mind kept swinging back to the Maxima.

On the way home, I barely saw the dim streets and alleyways where I walked. I kept thinking, of course, about the show. About the girl, the band, and Django. But how much, I wondered, had been real, and how much had I imagined? Everything about Django was unreal, which doesn't mean it was fake or stupido or a bore. Just the opposite: Django was unreal the way lightning is—amazing, loud, dangerous, freaky. He was unreal like the best dream I ever had, or that picture of Earth that the Apollonauts sent back when they walked on the Moon, or the feeling you get when somebody looks you right in the eyes, and it's like she can see all the way through you, or down deep into the deepest part of who you are.

He was—as the kids with the rhinestones had said—like a god. He'd come down to earth and then gone back to the heavenly realms of stars. But the girl, I kept telling myself, was more like me. We had at least one thing in common—fan-madness. And she might not have come from out of town for the show. I might, somehow, find her.

Up ahead the Angelus loomed. It had slender spires like a medieval church, massive turrets like a fortress, and a thousand windows. At that hour, most were dark. But in a hotel that vast—and it was the biggest in the city—someone is always awake. The Angelus took up an entire block, on one side the balconies hanging over the Great Canal, and on the other, hundreds of rooms facing the grandest boulevard in the city. The main entrance would've served well at a baron's or prince's palace. I went around the side, not wanting the desk staff to see me come in that late.

The buzzing, dreamy concert feel kept going as I snuck through the southwest servants' entrance and into the main kitchen.

"What are you doing up this late, Davi?" Maria-Claire's voice was soft and low. She was sitting in the shadow, waiting I supposed, for an important late night order to come in on the hotel intercom. I wouldn't call her pretty, and her hair had a few streaks of gray. Still, she was the most graceful person I knew. She served food day and night, night and day, yet there was a charm, almost an elegance about her.

"I was hungry. I thought I'd get some . . ." I didn't bother finishing my lie.

She knew me too well to be fooled. I could trust her though, and that night she didn't press me for the truth. She'd been a maid, then a waitress, and now worked room service for the most costly suites in the northwest wing. The guest rooms there were the best in the hotel and so, usually, were the tips that Maria-Claire got. She'd worked there since before I was born and, of all the staff at the Angelus, was the one person I could count on the most.

So we sat a little while, picking at a slice of cold pizza caccia nanza. We didn't say much that night. We never did, really. And that was one of the reasons I liked being with her. No gossip, no small talk. She was sort of like a mother to me, but without the prying questions and annoying suggestions. I suppose that made her the best mother in the world: giving me great food, covering for me when I got in trouble, and never once giving me a look of disapproval.

"It's late," I said. "I really should be in bed."

"That's for sure. It's almost two," she said. "Good night, Davi." I'm not sure why, but there was always a little sadness in her voice.

I went up three stories on the staff elevator then got off and climbed a spiral stairway to the seventh floor. Mine was a long corridor with threadbare carpets. Once, long before, the pattern had shown tangled vines, palm trees, flowers of paradise, and birds with human faces. Now the carpets were so thin the wooden floor underneath showed through, and the pattern was barely visible, like figures seen in a fog.

The knobs sticking up from the banister posts were carved in the shape of spiky fruit. The light fixtures, too, had forms from nature: finger-like leaves, pine cones, swollen branches. There was an elevator in the old days, but the shaft had been empty for years. When I was little, I would sometimes look into the shaft, through the pebbled glass of the door, through the crisscross folding metal screen, and see the dim daylight falling like drizzle from above.

FOUR

Waking up after the show, I was still in a daze, unsure, unclear, woozy, and weak. I heard the bells of St. Florian's, first at noon, then one o'clock, before I got out of bed. My rooms were in the oldest wing of the Angelus, on the seventh floor. Being that far up, and having windows that faced out to the east, I could see the sun rise over the city if I wanted to. If I got up early enough, I could see dawn break over St. Florian's with its twin steeples, then the Duce's Dome, the Bridge of Tears, and even a little glimpse of the Maxima, down by the Great Canal.

That afternoon I didn't listen to any of the albums. I knew it wouldn't be as good as live, or it would blur what I remembered of the sound and the feel. Of course, I knew that soon enough I'd go back and listen another thousand times. But for a day or two, I wanted to hold onto what I had, in my brain and in my hands and the bones of my skull.

So I got out my stack of *Creedos* and went through them, looking at all the pictures. There was one cover story that showed the whole band: Rudy Lasher on gamba, Simon Faruk on baryton, Mick St. Clair on drums. And Django clutching the mic stand like he was getting electrocuted.

He had carrot-orange, fuzz-spike hair and wore a see-through shirt and tight snakeskin pants. Even though he was definitely a guy, there was something pretty—almost beautiful—about him. Lighter than air, hot and cool, above and *beyond*. He was a gorgeous, first-class freak, but he was *my* freak, even if there'd been five thousand fans screaming his name the night before. He was *mine*—when I had my door closed and a towel under it to block out the light, and when I had the headphones clamped tight on my ears and the Reptiles' riffs were coming hard and fast, bright as mirror-shine.

That year, I'd read all I could find about Django, in fanzines and music papers. *Creedo* did a cover story about him when the "Moon" tour started. I bought two copies, one to keep and one to cut up for the pictures. And there was Django, taped up on the back of my bedroom door, when I woke the next day with the noon sun making a fever glow on the backs of my amber silk curtains. He'd watched all night as I slept, and he was there when I got up.

Django Conn wasn't his real name. According to *Creedo*, it was something normal. But he made the true mutation and turned himself into Django Conn, and it was like there'd never been the other, normal guy. He'd vanished, or maybe the day the Apollonauts walked on the moon, the world he came from had vanished. Django invented himself with his new name and did some records solo. Then he formed the band, the Albino Reptiles from Dimension X, though everybody just called them the Reptiles. They put out *Gimme Back My Phantom Limbs* then *Man in the*

Moon in the Man. And that's when it all started to happen: the write-ups in *Creedo*, radio play, and the tour.

Lying there in bed, half in and half out of sleep, I had an uneasy thought. What if the girl hadn't really existed until I saw her at the show? What if she wasn't really there until I noticed her? I don't mean that I dreamed her out of nothing. But what if I somehow called her up, conjured her to be there? Not exactly like a black magic conjuration, but just because I wanted her to be there, she'd appeared. Or maybe another way of seeing it would be like alchemy. A pinch of white powder into the flask, a glug of sour-smelling yellowy goo, some milky stuff, and a handful of black, crumbled crystals. Then turn on the flame underneath. Maybe it would boil over all frothy or suddenly turn perfectly clear and calm. And there she was, conjured up.

It doesn't quite make sense anymore, but that was the way my mind was working the morning after the show. Django was the alchemist. The music and the lights were the heat, and his lyrics were the spells. And all the fans packed into the Maxima were the secret ingredients to make something that had never been before.

FIVE

If every room at the Angelus was booked, the hotel could have held over five hundred guests. That, in my memory, had never happened. Business was still good though. And when I wandered through the lobby, there were usually people arriving or leaving with their small mountains of baggage. Uniformed porters stood ready to carry the bags. Either Armand or Arthur, who I swear were twins, welcomed new guests at the main desk. The concierge, with a pink carnation in his lapel, waited in his office to assist in any way he could. Money flowed, phones rang, long-term residents and overnight guests came and went.

My great grandfather had founded the Angelus. My grandfather had expanded it to its current size and made it the most famous hotel in the city. My father had run the Angelus his whole life. But things had changed since the glory days, when dukes and prime ministers and princes of the Church had stayed here. I'd heard rumors that my father was selling his shares slowly, losing control as the city changed, and the hotel business changed with it.

Something new, something powerful, like the swell of a midnight tide, had come moving into the city. Some people, such as my father, denied it was real. They kept on pretending that things would always be the same. Some people, my sister Sabina for instance, thought it had to do with ghosts and ancient waking spirits. And some people—like the girl with the glasses and me—opened our eyes and ears and said yes.

Something new was happening. That much everyone understood, though nobody talked about it. Tourists still flooded into the city, spending money and their time among the old decaying churches and shrines. The Crimson Carnival would always be a huge draw for gawkers and true believers. The Great Rites of St. Florian still brought in thousands of travelers and sightseers each spring. The biggest film festival on the continent attracted celebrities from around the world. And of course there was the old concert music that pulled people to the city. Vivaldi, Verdi, von Weber had their loyal followers. When they weren't being played at the Maxima, however, then Django Conn or the Starry Crowns, V-Rocket, the Witch-Babies or the Invisible Boys might be found there blasting away at the Old World shadows.

SIX

Glam and glister had swept over the continent just the year before. The most famous bands in the world all of a sudden seemed deader than Tosca and Toscanini. That was a big part of the change. Stars who'd been huge, selling millions of albums and filling the biggest stadiums, looked old and sounded fake. But there was more to it than just new bands with wild hair and capes, kids wearing turquoise amulets and gobs of purple makeup.

Mostly it was signs. In the ancient High Church days, people saw them in the heavens. The sun would turn blood-red, comets would appear as warnings of war or disaster, stars would fall, wailing from the sky. It was like that, but not exactly, because no one knew how to interpret these new signs. I heard rumors of winds from the eastern deserts carrying poisonous dust. What did that mean? No one could say for sure. The dolphins in the Fountain of Poseidon, in the grand piazza, turned overnight from bright bronze to charred black. No explanation made sense. Messages and quavering pictures—like something seen under water—appeared on people's TV screens. The Great Zeppelin of the North was blown off course by an icy December storm and disappeared. The Apollonauts had landed on the moon, harvested their magic rocks, and headed back. This world where I lived would never be the same once boots had walked in the lunar dust and gloved hands had poked in the piles of moon rubble.

At least that's how it felt the night we all stayed up until three o'clock to see the silver machine come down from blackness and settle in that stony crater. Most people had gathered together for parties, watching the final approach and moon landing on big screens. My father had put on a huge celebration in the hotel ballroom. Champagne flowed and cigars made a swirling blue cloud. Sabina had gone with her friends to see actors put on a show of the landing on the Maxima stage, exactly as it was happening two hundred thousand miles away. I'd stayed in my room and watched it all by myself. I turned the sound on the TV off and put on the Starry Crowns' first album. Exactly as the lander's retro-fires hit the lunar surface, my favorite song broke from the speakers. Cold ringing gamba-riffs and the girl-boy voice filled my room and my brain as the six metal feet touched down on the moon.

And the next day, when the Apollonauts finally opened up the hatch and stepped out, was the first time I heard the Witch-Babies' new song "Raving and Craving." I was looking out my window, over the city, when the song's riff came churning through my headphones. The sun was out, bright and hot, but I was safe inside my room, standing behind the curtains.

The change began before the sun had gone down. There was a new guy telling the news, or maybe it was the old one, but they'd done something to make him look different. His hair was darker and longer. His eyes were a sharp, metallic green. He even talked in a different way, using some words that I'd never heard before: *parallax, widdershins, sidereal.* There were commercials for brand new products with connections to the Apollonaut mission. Astro-foods, cosmic drinks, a hairstyle called the Artemis (named after the ancient goddess of the moon).

And Django Conn came like a comet streaking across the sky. The biggest, the brightest, the best thing I'd ever seen.

SEVEN

I'd always had two rooms at the Angelus, on the seventh floor: numbers 777 and 779. My sister Sabina was down the hall in 783 and 785. Between us, when we were younger, was our duenna. But she was gone now. It had been three years ago, when Sabina turned fifteen, that she announced to everyone that there was no point anymore in having a creaky, nearsighted black-dress hag-lady to watch over us.

So the room between stayed empty. At the end of the hall was another suite, abandoned for years. It had been set up for our schooling with a blackboard, two big oak tables, crowded bookshelves, and even some old equipment for science experiments. There was a stuffed monkey, pickled frogs floating in big glass jars of formaldehyde, and a collection of sea shells from around the world. For our anatomy lessons, our father had bought us a real human skeleton. We'd named him "The Monsignor" and dressed him up in a long red robe.

Sabina liked reading, especially books about mythical beings, spiritual secrets, séances, theosophy, and lost lore. I didn't mind learning history and music. But between Sabina's vicious tongue and my daydreaming, we'd made life miserable for every one of our tutors, and they never lasted long. Eventually our father gave up trying to get us properly educated, and the room had been unused ever since.

So I was left alone with my records and my stacks of fan mags. And Sabina could do as she pleased, which lately meant having séances and tarot card readings in her room. Mostly, I thought Sabina's talk about psychic powers and spirit-guides was not much more than a joke. But sometimes, especially when I'd done something I shouldn't have, it felt like she could see into my thoughts. She claimed that she was clairvoyant—that she could actually see things that weren't there in front of her eyes. And when I was little, she'd tell me that she'd looked around inside my head and knew all the bad thoughts I had. She hadn't bothered with that in a while. I didn't believe it anymore, but still, it spooked me when I remembered her giving me that I-know-everything-about-you look.

EIGHT

That afternoon, lying around paging through my stack of *Creedos*, I heard footsteps and voices in the hallway. This was odd, because normally Sabina had no visitors in the daytime. And other than Gio, who'd been the desk clerk at the Angelus when my grandfather was the owner, we had the whole corridor to ourselves. Gio stayed in his room, listening to operas on the radio. Weeks would go by without us ever seeing him. The maids checked in on him to make sure he was still alive, and one of the old waiters would bring him his supper on a zinc-plated cart. Other than that, our hallway was usually as desolate as the tombs of St. Sebastian.

I assumed at first it was just some adventurous kids who'd wandered off from the main guest wings. Then I thought it might be a couple of new laundresses who'd snuck away from the basement to steal a cigarette break and didn't know that anyone lived in this corridor. They were girls' voices, however they didn't seem secretive or worried. And one of them laughed, high and loud and unafraid of being caught. Then I heard a guy—it was Carlos, my sister's boyfriend—knock on a door and say,

"Come on. Open up, Sabina. It's us." After a minute, he knocked again, louder.

The door to Number 783 opened, and Sabina let them in. Then silence for a long time. But eventually I heard something that might have been music. Low and steady, a swelling current of chords, like an organ prelude in the cathedral. I knew my mind had been seriously shaken up by Django and the band. The girl with the glasses, of course, remained in my thoughts—a glimmer, a ghost, a strobe-lit face.

The Angelus too, the huge building itself, sometimes made sounds that were almost music. The radiators moaned slithery, Middle Eastern melodies in the winter months. The wind, now and then, came off the canals and filled the Angelus with a sad, solemn chorus. Doves cooed in the eaves, the elevator cables made a gigantic three-note groaning, and the water pipes sang like far-off spirits. This sound from my sister's room was not anything I'd heard before. So I did something that I hardly ever allowed myself to do anymore. After getting dressed quickly, I snuck into the room between to eavesdrop on Sabina and her guests.

NINE

Listening in secret was one of my favorite things to do. And having lived my whole life at the Angelus, I knew a hundred ways to get close to other people, to eavesdrop, without them knowing I was there. Sabina had caught me a few times, and we'd made a deal: she wouldn't tell and I wouldn't sneak around behind her with secret ears. The room between was part of our arrangement. We'd both agreed to leave it as a buffer, a dead zone between us.

But a change had happened: in me, in the Angelus, in the city. Since Django's show, everything felt different. The rules I'd gone by for years hadn't been totally thrown away, but I understood them differently now. And if Sabina was going to change—having guests in her room in the daytime—then I could change too.

I used the key that no one knew I had and entered the abandoned room. It smelled of dust, of rust, and of old lady lilac perfume. The curtains were drawn, making a blurred, reddish afternoon gloom. The bed had never been stripped, and the desk still had a crystal vase holding the dried bones of a very dead rose.

Going to the closet, I edged the door open just enough

to get inside and put my ear to the listening spot I'd made years before. The music was definitely coming from next door. It wasn't so mysterious now: a reedy little organ making soft minor church chords. And a voice was speaking something that might have been a prayer.

I'd spent my whole life in a city full of churches, but only been to mass a few times. Our father had to get along with the Archbishop and the monsignors who ruled. So he showed respect and paid the right tithes to the right accounts. A few times a year, he attended services at St. Florian's, paying with his time, with his kneeling and bowing, another kind of debt to the Archbishop. I liked the spicy traces that clung to his clothes when he came home from church: burnt sandalwood, myrrh, frankincense. Other than the change in the tolling of the bells, however, Sundays were no different at the Angelus than any other day. All of this is to say I didn't know much about religion, and I cared even less. The old music, the capes and crowns, the robes and relics were beautiful. Gorgeous church spires and domes surrounded the Angelus. Still, religion itself didn't mean much at all to me.

So hearing what sounded like prayer from my sister's room was odd indeed. And even odder were the bursts of high, riotous laughter, as though one of her other guests thought the whole thing was a joke or a ridiculous put-on. I leaned in closer to my listening spot, pressing my ear hard against the bare wood where I'd scraped off the plaster. At first, it was just a cloud of noise.

TEN

Then a girl's voice, darker and lower and more serious, came out of the blur.

"Impossible? So what? You're going to let that stop you?"

My listening spot was tight, hot, and airless. The closet smelled of old shoes and moth-eaten taffeta dresses. My knees already hurt and my ear was burning. Hearing those words, though, I felt a current of life flowing to me and through me.

"You know what else is impossible? Apollonauts landing on the moon, but they did it. Am I right? Not just landing on the moon, but coming back—all the way back through how many thousands of miles of absolute nothing?—and landing here in the ocean with a box full of rocks they took from the moon. I saw one with my very own eyes, a rock that came all the way from the moon. It didn't look any different than any other rock I'd ever seen. But I knew what it was and I knew where it came from, and it was absolutely impossible and absolutely true. So don't get all weak-kneed and worried about what other people are saying."

"But you don't have all the facts," Sabina said. "When you understand better, then you'll see—"

The other voice cut her off, not angry, just impatient, wound-up with excitement. "I see just fine. I understand just perfect. If you really want your ritual to be true, then it is. Don't tell me you're serious and then go all giggly and imbecilo on me. Carlos said you were serious, and I thought he meant it."

"Of course I did," Carlos said. "I had a good feeling about you and how you'd fit in here." Depending on her mood, how grand and pretentious she was feeling, Sabina called Carlos her boyfriend, her soul mate, or her spiritual advisor. He was a few years older than her, confident and cool, supremely good-looking, and she'd fallen for him hard. She thought she was Mistress Sophisticato now, having her séances and swanning around with him.

The girl started up again. "You can light candles and sing your cute little woo-woo spirit-songs and tell yourselves that you're raising the angels from their secret places. But if you're not serious then I'm going."

The voice stopped suddenly. I heard the rustling of cloth and a chair being dragged across the floor. For a long second I thought that I'd been found out. I held my breath, straining to hear what was going on. The girl started up again at last, with an edge to her voice that hadn't been there before.

"You're doing it all wrong. Church music only works if you believe it. Consecrated wine? It's just wine. And stealing holy water from the Dome? It's just water that a priest muttered over. But if you want to raise some power then you've got to take some risks. You need the real and true things: blood, fire, moonlight, and music."

The girl sounded totally sure of herself. She knew what was real and what was fake. She knew and she had nothing to lose by saying it.

"So if you want to make the mutation, then good. I'm in. All the way in. I'll stay around and show you what it means to make the change. But if you're just going to . . ."

ELEVEN

The voice died. Maybe the girl turned suddenly or moved away, or somebody made a sign to silence her. Other voices, much more muffled, came and went. I heard a sudden wheezing outburst of notes, as if the girl had leaned her elbow on the keyboard. Something metal, a cup or plate, dropped on the floor. Footsteps, the rattle of something, probably Sabina's little divining bones, being dropped into a jar, and my sister telling the others to stop talking.

Then I heard a knock on Sabina's door. Panicking, I pulled myself out of the closet and crossed the middle room. I listened, holding my breath, heard nothing and slipped out. Back in my room, I felt safer but my heart was still pounding.

Soon, I heard my sister's door open and her guests heading down the hallway to the stairs. They were talking, but too quietly for me to make out a word.

I wanted to see. I had to see. Voices are fine. But sound and sight together makes something real. So, still buzzed on the adrenaline of secrets and panic, I opened my door and took a peek. Three people were moving together toward the stairs. One was separate, lagging a little behind. Wild black hair, tight crimson jeans, some kind of Arctic-white jacket. And even though I couldn't see her face, I knew it was the girl, the one from the Maxima, the one who'd been talking about Sabina's rituals being fake. She was there in my hallway, but moving away from me, into shadow.

The sight of her hit me like a jolt of two hundred-volt Django-juice. It didn't hurt, but it came close. It didn't scare me but almost. It was like magnetism, maybe, both negative and positive, an invisible push and pull. I wanted to yell out to her, "Hey! It's me. I was at the show too." And at the same time, I wanted to close my door and hide.

Carlos, wearing a silver-studded vest and silver-heeled boots, hung back, waiting for her. He said something I didn't catch, then I heard some names: *Luigi, Lukas, Santa Lucia, Jules.* All the names blurred together, a cloud of *oohs* and liquid *L's*.

I was never sure how to take Carlos. He pretended to like the new bands sometimes, at least when Sabina wasn't around. He claimed that he'd hung out with the Invisible Boys after a show. Was this true or false? I never found out. He'd traveled and he seemed to know a lot about a lot of things. He showed me an autographed copy of *Red Chaos* by Hakim Hakim. And it was the real thing. Still, there was always a sliminess about Carlos. It was more than the fact he couldn't tell the truth: I never really understood what he wanted from me. Or why.

He turned, saw me, and gave me a smirky smile, as though to say, "Back way off, kid. Don't even think about messing with this."

For a second, I thought he was going to put his arm

around the girl's shoulder, but she veered away from him. I heard him say "D'Annunzio," which was the street on the east side of the Angelus. He gave me his king-of-the-world warning sneer and went with the girls to the elevator. Another second or two, and then they were gone.

I headed the other direction, to the back spiral stairway.

TWELVE

Knowing the ins and outs of the Angelus better than anyone, I made it down to the ground floor before them. I went through the kitchen and dining room and into the main lobby. Though I'd grown up here and had never known another home, sometimes I still got a little flicker of joy when I entered the lobby and saw the huge chandeliers, the ranks of sofas and black enameled tables, the broad stairways and alcoves where people lounged and met, waited and read their magazines, drank bitter coffee from beautiful silver cups, nibbled glazed chocolates, and made slow elegant clouds of smoke with their Turkish cigarettes.

Today I had only one thing on my mind: following the girl, hoping she'd get rid of Carlos.

The elevator doors came open with a hissing sigh. Carlos got out, then the girl from the concert, and last was the other girl—the one I didn't know—who said goodbye and went to the coffee shop just off the lobby.

I wasn't hiding—not exactly. Sometimes I thought I didn't need to hide as I snuck around the hotel, that I was almost invisible. Today, I just stayed back, hung around with others, blended into the background.

Carlos pointed to the hallway that led to D'Annunzio Boulevard. He was pouring on the charm, though it didn't seem that the girl was paying much attention. She stared at the opulence of the lobby, stood there a minute just soaking up the overload of gold, silver, and bronze; of silk, damask, and satin.

Smooth as the maitre d' of a great restaurant, puffed-up like the conductor of a world-class orchestra, Carlos gestured for the girl to go with him out to the street. They were talking, though I could barely understand any of the words. *Luigi, Lukas, Santa Lucia, Jules.* The names they'd mentioned upstairs came back to me again: *L's* and *oohs*, floating in my mind.

I cut through a utility hallway, a narrow passage that guests never saw, and came out into sunshine on the east side of the hotel. For a second I panicked, thinking that Carlos had seen me and headed off another way. But then the doors opened and out they came.

He was still talking. She was silent.

THIRTEEN

Something had changed in those few minutes while I'd lost sight of them. The girl was shaking her head, backing away. Carlos was trying to keep his cool, still using his slickest voice. He'd said or done the wrong thing, though, and she was making it obvious now that she wanted him to leave her alone.

"You're sure you don't want to—"

"I'm sure," she said. "Absolutely positively."

He gave up with a shrug and a suave smile. I heard him say, "We'll see you tomorrow?" Without answering, she turned and headed down the street.

Carlos went back into the hotel, and I didn't need to keep hidden anymore. The girl hadn't noticed me at the show. Why would she? What she'd gone through at the Maxima was pure Django-possession. I'd just been one more nameless, faceless body floating nearby. Even if I'd slammed into her and screamed in her face, she wouldn't have noticed me the night before.

So it should have been easier now to follow her.

And for a little while I did fine, watching her move down the sidewalk, wondering what she was looking at in the store windows, trying to conjure a name for her in my mind. Something plain? Something exotic? None of the names I called up from memory, and tested out, seemed right. I pretended, in my head, to introduce myself. "Hi, I'm Davi. I was at the show." I thought about racing right up to her and grabbing her arm. But that was wrong too.

I suppose I was still a bit blurry-brained from the night before, and definitely playing with the names made me lose concentration. I saw her go into a little boutique jewelry store. She came out then went back in again, as though she'd forgotten something.

Then she went quickly down the street, and I hurried to catch up with her. Or maybe it wasn't her who'd come out the second time. There weren't many girls on the street with her look—wild hair, sphinx-skin jeans and creamy silk jacket—but the crowds there were pretty heavy, and the bright sunshine was messing up my vision.

I was running now, trying to catch a glimpse. The crowds on the street got denser and pushed back against me, like a tide coming in. I saw her—I think—turn down an alleyway. By the time I'd gotten there, she was gone.

FOURTEEN

I stood there panting, feeling one hundred percent imbecilo. Why hadn't I just gone up to her as soon as she'd gotten rid of Carlos? Why hadn't I shouted out for her? Maybe it would've made me look like a fool. But at least I'd have had a chance. Now, there were an infinite number of places for me to look.

Countless streets, nameless alleys, tiny apartments and huge cathedrals, crowded bridges, empty promenades, piazzas and theaters, galleries and salons and palaces: the city was for me as big as an entire world.

The most logical spots for me to look were the record shops. So I went a few blocks, crossed the St. Paulus bridge and down a narrow street crowded with antique shops and stuffy little coffee houses. There, tucked between a chapel and a two-chair barber, was a place where sometimes I bought albums. And there was Luigi, leaning on the counter, staring at a tiny TV. The place was small enough that he could watch for shoplifters from his place behind the cash register. There was no crowd of sticky-fingered kids that day, though. Besides Luigi, I was only person in the shop. He looked up for a second. I'm sure he recognized me, because I'd spent plenty of money there. But his greeting wasn't much more than a nod. "Luigi," I said to myself. He had to be the one Carlos had been talking about. Maybe this was where he met her.

"Have you seen a girl?" I asked. "She's got wild-looking hair. And glasses. She's really into Django Conn. You know her?"

Luigi considered this for a second or two, then went back to his TV without even answering.

"I'm looking for her. It's really important." I surprised myself, saying this. "She was at the show last night. I need to find her."

"Sure," Luigi said. "Five thousand kids. Sure. I remember everybody." He took a heavy drag, blew clove-scented smoke at me, and ground out his cigarette as though wanting to grind me out. "Now, you want to buy something today or did you just come around to—"

FIFTEEN

The bell on the door jingled, and a guy who didn't seem to belong there came in. I don't mean he looked confused or lost. It was more that he didn't fit in. After about five seconds, it was pretty obvious he wasn't there to buy the new V-Rocket album or pick up the latest fan-mag. No, it was *somebody*, not *something* he was looking for.

His eyes were like two inky holes. At least, that was what it seemed like as he turned to look at me. Not just deep, dark brown, but truly moonless, midnight black. I didn't notice what he was wearing, because it was the face, the look, that went straight into my brain. Just for a fleeting flick of a moment, I thought the look was about hate, real loathing. Only I'd never seen him before. So why would he hate me? And then I thought maybe it was the opposite. But I was nothing to look at. Why would anybody with that kind of intensity even notice me, let alone care?

I thought later that other people probably turned and stared at him all the time. He was that good-looking, like a film star who'd just stepped out of the movie screen. So maybe he was just giving me what he always got, but in reverse. It was a fierce gaze: sort of an attack to defend himself. Supposedly, other faces can be like mirrors. I'd read that in a *Creedo* interview Django gave. He said we look into other people's faces and see ourselves, or what we're feeling. It didn't make much sense, but that's what it seemed like when the guy stared at me.

What did he see? I'm not sure. Boy or girl, plain or beautiful, rich or poor: he didn't care about those. There was something else he looked for inside me, like an x-ray camera searching for secrets. But he didn't find any, at least not then. He was about to say something, I think, but changed his mind. He gave up on me, as though I was a bug he'd found interesting for a second or two. He glanced around the shop quickly then headed for the door. Luigi shrugged and looked up at me, as if asking without speaking whether I was going to spend any money that day.

It took me a minute to calm down, to remember where I was and why. Should I stay, I wondered, waiting around to see if the girl showed up? Should I just wander from store to store, street to street, letting luck take me where I needed to go? Or should I give up right then, this impossible search to find someone whose name I'd never heard, and who had no idea that I even existed?

SIXTEEN

Back on the street, I told myself to just give up and go home. This was stupido, a total, embarrassing waste of time. The longer I spent wandering around, the worse I was going to feel when I got back to my rooms. Luck had given me my one chance, and I'd blown it.

Then, at the end of the street, I thought I saw her again. Just a quick glimpse, like a flash of movement in the corner of my eye. There and then gone, into a doorway. One more try, I told myself. One more time chasing the black and red girl-ghost.

It was another record store, and I'd messed up again. She wasn't there.

Like at the last place, there was only one other customer. This one was a kid with a wild green-gold shag haircut, turquoise jumpsuit, and platform-heeled shoes. Of course it couldn't be, but I thought at first it was the guy I'd just seen at Luigi's. Somehow he'd made a transformation, and gotten to the next store ahead of me. I stared at him, a little woozy and weak in the legs. He stared back, as though I was the one who was out of place. I saw then that it was somebody new, somebody I'd never run into before, though like the guy with the inky black eyes, there was something a little off about him.

It seemed odd to see a glister-boy, in full Django-drag, at that time of day. Especially since the boy was alone. In a gang of other kids, it would've seemed somehow more right, or safer. At the Maxima there'd been hundreds of them, like a flock of birds with the same splendid plumage. But with the late afternoon sun shining in the shop windows, it seemed too open, too bold. I'd never played with dressing that way, in public or in private. No makeup, no lipstick, no mascara. No gold lame or silvery chiffon. I'd stare for hours at the record covers and color pictures in *Creedo*, imagining what it would feel like to have such a look. Boy-girl, both-neither, fake-real, yes and no. Wild, outrageous, way beyond, and free. But I never once crossed the line and tried to imitate Django.

I glanced over at the bin the kid was looking through. The Sabbath-Breakers, the Salamanders, Sergeant Silvero, Sigmund Boyd, Sweet Tooth: these bands were okay, but nothing compared to Django and the Reptiles. I went to *his* bin and flipped through the records. I had everything, but it felt good to see the albums in their shiny plastic wrappers, sealed up tight. Four copies of *Man in the Moon in the Man*. Five of *Gimme Back My Phantom Limbs*. A New World import version of "Stellar Bodies" and six copies of Django's first record, when he was still a solo act. It felt good to see so many of his faces, different looks from album to album, and the same cover pictures lined up four, five, six in a stack.

There was an espresso bar down the street where

sometimes I'd see glister kids gathered. That day there were just two old men there, playing dominoes and listening to the sad wail of Madama Butterfly. I peeked into a church where somebody was getting married or having a funeral, but I didn't stay long enough to find out which it was. Crossing the Bridge of Tears, I looked into the oozy, black canal. The sun made a long, blood-red wound in the surface of the water. A boat went by, moving slowly, almost drifting. It broke up the play of light, and I moved on, ending up over near the Duce's Dome, standing in line to see a movie.

It was a B-grade horror flicker from the New World called something like *Daughter of the Shadows*, or *Darkness and the Girl*. I didn't pay much attention to the name or who was starring in it. There was a gloomy, gothic castle of course, and lightning bolts, and big swells of overloaded orchestral music. The girl in the movie had crazy, wild eyes, and I think some kind of powers that let her see what no one else could see.

In the film, there was another world, I think. A world that overlapped this one, or crossed through it the way clouds of smoke cross the sky but the things behind are still visible. She could go back and forth, I think, or talk to people in both worlds. And of course no one took her seriously until the end when it all came crashing together. But the movie had pretty good special effects, and so, at least for the two hours I sat in the darkness of the theater, I almost believed it.

SEVENTEEN

The movie finished and I walked out. Giving up the search and watching the movie had calmed me down. It was okay, I told myself. Maybe I could ask Sabina who the girl was. Or I might run into her again at another show.

Maybe it was letting go that did the trick. Good luck, dumb luck, karma, surrendering to the totally random—whatever it was—I'd found her.

There she was, the girl with the glasses and the wild black hair. The girl I'd heard—from my secret place—talking about music and mutation. She'd been in the theater the whole time with me, watching and hearing, soaking up the shadows and the sounds. She was alone too. And like me, going from the black and white shadows to the pomegranate reds and lemon yellows of sunset, she was a bit unsure of herself, at least at first.

"Why are you following me?" she asked.

"What do you mean?" My words came out a little awkward, as they usually did.

She edged up closer, as though to get a better look at me. "Following me. I saw you go into Luigi's earlier. Then over on San Mateo. And now here." She didn't seem angry, just confused. "What's going on?"

"I saw you at the show." No intro, no small talk. "Django Conn." She gave me an off-kilter look. "The Maxima. Last night. The Albino Reptiles from Dimension X." I started right in, which was something I hardly ever did, talking to a girl like that.

She looked at me like she didn't believe anything I'd said. So I rattled off the songs from the show, and the names of the Reptiles, and described what Django had been wearing, to prove to her that I'd really been there. "He's the greatest."

"Absolutely," she said, relaxing a little. "The greatest."

"My name's Davi."

She waited just a couple of seconds, then said, "I'm Anna Z."

That was the shortest thing I ever heard her say. Soon enough, so many words were coming out of her that I felt like I was drowning. Wild stories, charming lies, true facts and fairy tales, rambling rants, song lyrics, rhymes and riddles and beautiful secrets. But for those couple of minutes, she still didn't know if she could trust me. So she didn't say much at first.

I asked about her favorite album. Of course, like me, it was *Man in the Moon in the Man*. We agreed that it was amazing and that we could listen to it a thousand times and never use it up. Only ten songs and there was a whole world hidden there in the grooves.

"Radiation Nation," I said.

"Signs and Wonders," she said back. "With the wild gamba solo, right?"

"Love and Gravity, Royal Shining Things," I said the song names like I was using secret passwords. "Forty Months and a Day. The first time I heard that one, I thought my brain was going to catch on fire."

She didn't walk away saying I was a freak or an imbecilo turd-toy. I'd been through that enough times before, people telling me to go away, that I was too fanatical, too wound-up, too much. But right there in front of the theater, I went up to her and started talking about Django Conn, and that's all it took to bring us together.

"I've got some bootleg LPs and some really rare 45s," I told her, not bragging, but saying it just to see how she'd respond. "I saw a ticket stub from his first show with the Reptiles. A guy had it for sale. It was supposedly autographed, but how could you prove that Django really signed it?"

I kept thinking how amazing it was that she didn't walk away. Once she'd gotten used to me, and that didn't take long, she stood there like she was really listening. And I did too. Of course, that was probably easier for me because she was Anna Z, and there was nobody like her on the whole planet, maybe in the whole universe. Her hair wasn't quite so wild as at the Maxima, but there were still black snakes tangled in it. No liquid blurs of color moved on her glasses. All the same, it was hard to see her eyes. Swept up into Django's sound, she was lost and found. Standing on the street with me, she wasn't so free, so spontaneous. But I remembered how she'd been, and I knew she'd be that way again.

I told her about the Angelus, that my family owned it

and that I had always lived there. I mentioned Sabina and Carlos and the others. And that was all it took to make the final link between us, because she told me she'd been there just a few hours before. It really was her I'd heard through the wall, talking about blood, fire, moonlight, music, and mutation. It was no phantasm I'd seen walking down the hallway to the elevator.

EIGHTEEN

"I met Carlos just a couple of days ago," she told me, as we headed for the Angelus. "I thought he was cool at first. And he knows everybody who's anybody. He said he had some friends who'd found 'a thin place between here and there.' That's how he put it, and it sounded like the real thing, not just kids playing around with Ouija boards and black candles. Not just fooling and faking but really going across the line to the Big Beyond. So I met up with them, just yesterday at Santa Lucia's, that's over by the Don Rodrigo canal, and we had cinnamon coffee and talked, and so *that's* your sister? She doesn't look anything like you. I don't mean she's not pretty, but she's dark and you're so pale. I can't believe that you two are really related."

It was like the words had been dammed up inside her, and with me around they broke loose in a huge, gushing wave. "I didn't like her at first, and I didn't like her any more after I went up to her room with those others. I'm not saying they're fake or total fools. They've got the goods. Carlos showed me some of his books, and your sister has a communion knife and a chalice she said came from St. Florian's. They're beautiful, real gold, I think. Or electrum—that's a mix of silver and gold. They really are amazing, and her friend Cyanne said she'd been to Aleister Crowley's secret place, the Abbey of Thelema. Carlos said he was there at Cape Canaveral when the Apollonauts took off for their third trip to the moon. And it all sounded so 'verily verily I say unto you heavy and true.' But then they started in with the séance, and it wasn't much more than a joke."

She went on like that the whole way back to the Angelus, talk pouring out of her. Sometimes it seemed like she was making herself up out of words, an endless stream of monologuing. She could go on for hours, and I loved to listen because her talk was better than any buzz a kid could get from smoking fly-spell or sniffing white gong. Sometimes it was like she got drunk on herself talk-talk-talking and I'd get a contact high from just listening.

"You must've done the rites with her, right? So you know. I don't have to explain anything. You know the difference between dynamite and a dishrag. You can tell Mars from marzipan. You saw Django live and you've heard the records and—Sweet Jesu with Jelly!—you know what kind of kiddie games they're up to. I couldn't believe it. All that great ritual stuff, and money to buy more I'm sure, and you live in the Angelus no less. That place is just amazing! I couldn't afford a room there for one night, and you've lived there your whole life! But they don't want to hear a thing about mutation music or life in the Real Outside. It was just ghosty-ghosty and woo-woo stupido."

NINETEEN

We went in through the Prince Eugenio foyer, and I took her straight through the grand lobby. She didn't care who saw her gawking or what they thought. She loved it, being there and seeing all the gilding and garnish, the bright lacquer and dark tapestries, the silk Renaissance hangings I went by every day, and the filigreed mirrors I hardly even saw anymore. She gaped at the luxury and rattled on about how amazing it was all the way to my room.

Earlier, she'd come in through one of the back entrances. Sabina and Carlos, I supposed, had told her to use the doorway that the maids and kitchen drudges used. It wasn't like she was a peasant from the countryside. She could talk about a hundred things that the pseudos my sister spent her time with had never even heard of. It was just that when she felt something, she let it loose. When she had a question, she asked it. And when she knew the truth, she said it out loud. I thought it was great that she didn't care how people judged her. She was free, absolutely free, and I wanted to be like that.

We took the elevator to the fourth floor then wandered the east wing, where I showed her the San Simeon ballroom and the conservatory. The heat and the sticky air always gave me a peculiar feeling. It seemed to affect her even more. The huge drooping leaves of all the exotic plants, the smells of black earth and overripe fruit combined to make a sweet, heady perfume. I showed her the coffee trees, the orchids heavy with swollen purple flowers, wormwood from Kashmir, sloe bushes from Lapland, and Illyrian blood oranges. We took our time there, and I think she got a little buzzed from all the scents and green secretions.

So it was dark by the time we got to my rooms. She flopped down on the bed and I asked her, "What do you want to hear?"

"You said you've got some good bootlegs."

I showed her all of them, one at a time, albums with plain white covers or ones cheaply printed in the New World. Mostly these bootlegs were live shows that somebody recorded secretly off the mixing board. A few had studio cuts that had never been released. Those were my faves. They seemed more private to me, like I'd snuck a peek into Django's mind and seen things he didn't want the rest of the world to see. I put on *The Great Conn*; we listened a while, and then she started talking again, making her worlds of words.

TWENTY

"Here's the way I see it. Music makes the mutation. Songs and riffs and Django's voice—all together, they're the mutagen. You know what that word means? You understand? The mutagen is the thing that makes a creature start changing into something new, like a weird science chemical or cosmic x-rays or the full moon that turns the werewolf into his true self. Or the radioactive spider-bite. Or the mummy's curse when the tomb is opened up after four thousand years. It's anything that makes the body mutate. Cells start changing and making new ones like crazy. And soon enough you've got yourself a real mutant on your hands. Like Django, and me. And you."

She flipped through a copy of *Creedo* and pointed to a picture showing Django and the band. It must've been shot through a filter or some gauze, because it gave all four of them a misty, see-through look.

"I'm telling you, Davi, he's the next step in human evolution. There was *Homo erectus*, which means the caveman who stood up straight, right? And there's *Homo sapiens*, which means the smart man. Which is what people are supposedly now. And we're *Homo lux*. Humans made out of light just like in the movies and the late show on TV. That's Django—and that's us too. You listening to me? You and me: we're the next step—higher and wilder, brighter and better, *beyonder* than all the rest.

"You've got to think like Dr. Frankenstein, Davi, if you really want to get it. Mad science experiments, secret formulas, graveyard hunting, lightning to give the life. Sneaking around in moonlight, ancient books, lost at the North Pole. Mad, wild science. But listen, the word 'science' means 'wisdom,' not just bubbling test tubes and electric switches and dials and rocket ships. It's about knowing, not just doing."

TWENTY-ONE

She lay back on the bed then and picked up the album sleeve for *Man in the Moon in the Man*. She held it like a mirror, seeing her own face in the shiny square. Because I left the cellophane on the record cover, there was a little gleam, a faint out-of-focus reflection.

"Listen to me, we're specters, Davi. S-P-E-C-T-E-R-S. And you know what that means? Not faked-up movieland ghosts. We're specters like Django and the Reptiles. You know what *specter* really means? The word comes from Latin. It means 'to look, to see, to spy on.' We're spies, Davi: flies on the wall and eyes in the sky. And there's the color spectrum too—all the shades shining together. There's spectacles. You know, the old word for eyeglasses. And there's prospectors, those old guys in the New World who go hunting for gold in the mountains. Get it? Pro-specters. We're searching for precious metals too. It's about looking and seeing what nobody else can see. You following me? We're spectacular, the new breed, and we will not stay hidden. We will be seen and heard. One day, we will show ourselves to the whole world. We're specters, Davi. S-P-E-C-T-E-R-S. And that's a good thing, the very best thing in the whole world."

She rolled onto her side and was quiet for a while, staring at me. At first I thought she'd changed her mind, realizing I wasn't as far gone as she was. I had all the things a fan, a true Django-fanatic, would have. But the way she talked, it was clear she'd gone way beyond, into a place I could hardly glimpse, let alone enter.

"Specters," I said, feeling like a fool. One word. That was the best I could do with her lying there on my bed. "Specters."

"Right. You got it," she said, and then started up again. "Something flickers on the screen and is it real? Just pictures or is it realer than real? You think that Frankenstein's creature or Dracula or the Wolfman aren't real? I don't mean you're going to see them boogying down the boulevard any time soon. But they're real in your brain, which is where it all happens. You can call them up and hear their voices and see them perfect and true. Do you think you're ever going to forget when the Bride of Frankenstein first sees her mate and starts that sexy, wild screaming? That's in your brain forever and ever. It was just a movie, right? Lights flickering on the screen and voices from a speaker. Just people made out of light and sound, like us, *Homo lux.* But they'll be around forever, long after every person you ever see today is long dead and long gone. Shadows and swirling smoke, silver gleams on the screen, and black and white fire like the torches of all those screaming peasants at the end of *Frankenstein,* when they come to get him and kill him but they never succeed. They can't ever really kill him because he's made out of light and sound and he comes back again and again and again. Just like you and me, Davi. You and me and Django, and all the wrong, true, beautiful, impossible specters."

TWENTY-TWO

We stayed in my room a long time that night, spinning records, looking at the covers, and talking. Or I should say that she talked and I listened. I had no clock because I had no reason to be anywhere at any particular hour. I never paid much attention to what time it was. Sometimes I noticed the church bells tolling, but they were more like background music than a reminder telling me I had to do something.

"You've got Django's first album, the one he made before he changed his name? You know about that, right? His first band was called the Soul Strangers. They were his first love when he was just a kid, our age, his first shot at the big time. They played blue slave music stolen from a lost river delta in the New World, like everybody else did in those days, white boys trying to be black men. He called himself 'The Crawling King Snake' and 'The High Priest Gone.' And he went. He disappeared. That's how it happened. He vanished, and then he came back as Django Conn, the Late Great Lord of Glister, the new Frankenstein."

There was a different look on her face when she talked about monster movies. Sadness, but the sadness that some people actually like to feel. Late autumn leaves have that sadness, and so does the look of a room after a great party is over, and some kinds of music too: slow and dreamy and deep as a goldmine.

"Remember? At first there was a rumor he came right out of the movie screen, like he was a special effect blend of Boris Karloff and Elsa Lanchester, Bela Lugosi and Carol Borland. Did you ever see her? She's great in *Mark of the Vampire*—cool, creepy, and beautiful. People said that Django was like a creature made up of all those stars. Vampire and mad scientist and werewolf. Witch and warlock, ghost and ghoul. But he's got something bigger, something ten thousand times more high voltage than horror movie stuff, and that's the voice, the words, the sound.

"You know, I'm still buzzing from the show. It was just last night, and it feels like it was a year ago, or in another life. I was really gone, really scrambled. I woke up this morning and it was like my whole body was a deck of cards that had been totally shuffled, dealt out, and played in some weird game. And I don't even know the rules. I was up front by the stacks. You said you saw me, right? I was practically close enough to touch him, and I felt the power surging off the stage, off of Django himself right into the crowd. Into me, myself, and I-don't-care! Everything was changing. Cells, germ plasm, brain spasm, molecules. I don't know what to call it, except everything was new and true, through and through, thank you, thank you, Sweet Jesu!"

Sometimes I think she was replaying songs from the deepest places in herself, the words and rhythms so much a part of who she was. And at other times they seemed more like messages.

TWENTY-THREE

It was past midnight, probably, when Anna Z got up off my bed and said she'd better be going.

"You want me to come with you?"

"Why?"

"I don't know. It's late. Things happen sometimes. Trouble."

"That's okay. I'll be fine. And anyway, it's a long walk," she said. "I live on the far side of the Black Lagoon. Over past the Hessian Quarter."

"So when are we getting together again?" I asked.

She said something vague about vespers at St. Florian's, then kissed me on my forehead. That's when my thoughts really started to melt down. Church and chimes. Songs and science and specters. They went churning in my brain. I needed to shut my eyes soon. I needed to be in bed. But after she'd left, I stood at the door, listening. I heard her footsteps and maybe the sound of a soft knocking down at the end. I opened my door a crack, peeking. The hallway was totally empty. The lights burned in their bronze ceiling sconces. The carpet extended all the way, like a great furry tongue, to the dark end of the corridor.

I went back to my stack of wax, knelt down, flipped through my fave albums, and found one I hadn't heard in a few months. I didn't care what it was, just something loud to push away my feelings. Excitement and fear, swirls of happiness, and shivers of confusion.

I'd grabbed the first album by the Starry Crowns, my fave band before I'd discovered Django Conn. With a shaky hand, I set the needle down into the groove and out came the chiming, galactic gamba-riff of "Praying for X-Rays." Usually, my nerves and my pulse calmed down when the music started. The best songs could do that for me. With the right chords, right tune, and right voices filling the space around me and inside me, the twisty backward-forward feelings would dwindle down to nothing, and I'd feel safe again.

I turned up the volume as the chorus came around again. Vance's voice was like a pale, gleaming tendril stretching across the emptiness of space. "Hear my whisper, hear my song. Praying for X-rays all night long."

TWENTY-FOUR

My fave writer for *Creedo* was a guy from the New World named T.V. Geist. He did record reviews, wrote snarky captions for the photos—like: "Neither bug spray or hair spray can save this man"—and usually one big article for every issue. Sometimes they were just the usual fan-mag trivia: gossip about the making of new albums, tour information for the biggest bands, interviews with stars who didn't really want to talk. But when T.V. had a subject he actually cared about, it showed. The words got wilder and the ideas went off in a hundred directions. Even though he was hard to follow then, he was really trying to make sense of something he really cared about.

I woke up even later than the day before and lay there in a daze. A couple dozen issues of *Creedo* were scattered on the floor around my bed. We'd been looking through them, but I didn't remember leaving such a mess. Of course, the mags were mostly open to articles about Django. One had a big photo spread showing him with his arms stretched and his head tilted back, the way St. Florian stood at the altar of his church. Another shot was of the whole band, wearing clothes that might have been made out of spider webs and a mummy's gauze wrappings.

The piece that went with the picture was called "He Came from Beyond—Maybe," and it was written by T.V. Geist. Though I'd read the article before, this time it made a lot more sense. Or maybe I just got more sense out of it. Mostly, T.V. went through all the rumors and guesses and theories about how Django came to be and who he really was.

Some people said he made himself into a human sacrifice, that he tore his own heart out of his chest and laid it still thumping on an ancient pagan altar. They said he poured out "his own warm, red blood as an offering to the gods whose names are many, yet never spoken."

Another theory claimed that he'd dissolved himself in psychedelic acid, one more longhair hipster casualty. That was how, supposedly, he made his transformation. "And thus the doors of perception opened unto him," T.V. wrote, "and he strolled right through, smirking and sparkling."

There were books that talked about conspiracies, mysterious medical operations, secret plots, and even murder. "Or maybe he just got offed by some cranked-up Metal fans." Alcohol, asthma, amphetamines: all of these got mentioned. Some people were positive he'd been found floating face down in the Great Canal the day the first Apollonaut had walked on the moon. "I even met one beautiful, young blonde bimbette," T.V. wrote, "who swore on a stack of blue Voovoo Bibles that the Great Conn was swept away in the monstrous beating of black, veiny wings."

TWENTY-FIVE

I wasn't sure how to take any of this. Sometimes T.V. would spin out long, complicated tales just for fun, or because the bands wouldn't give him any real stories to print. The biggest names were already rich and famous, so why should they pass on any hot gossip to the fan mags? And the ones that hadn't made it all the way to the top just wanted to look good. So the whole thing was always a bit of a maze. And sometimes I felt lost inside it, wandering, hoping to find my way out. Or at least a reason to be there.

That day, there was a different scent in the air, the after-trace of Anna Z. It wasn't like Sabina's spicy perfumes, or the smell of baking on the waitresses, or soap and clean sheets on the maids. I took a couple of deep breaths, almost like the kids who huffed white gong to get buzzed. Being with Anna Z had made me feel weird and free. Just a faint whiff of her and I was there again.

I went to the window and looked out. Beyond the roof-top, the afternoon sun gleamed on golden domes and silver spires. And church bells were pealing, an outburst as complicated as jungle drums. Anna Z had said we were people made of light and sound: *Homo lux.*

"I know, I know, either something's real or it's fake, right? Something can't be both. That's what everybody says. But most everybody is wrong most of the time. *Homo lux?* People made out of light and sound? That can't be. Either you're flesh and bones and skin and blood, or you're just made-up, fake, bogus, imaginary. That's all you hear, all the time. Unreal. Impossible."

I wondered now if the whole city was the same as that. Like a movie, like Django's show at the Maxima: voices and riffs, glister and glam, sound and light, and nothing more.

TWENTY-SIX

Sliding *Man in the Moon in the Man* out of its paper sleeve, I laid it carefully on the turntable and set the needle gently into the groove, at the second cut. Anna Z had said that "Flash Bang Baby" was the closest Django got to explaining what was happening and why. So I listened and listened, reading the words printed inside the album's gatefold cover.

> *Cold light—they came to save our souls*
> *a brave crew, who came with lives from golden*
> *true night—that's hovering high and solar*
> *a bright wave, that kneeling we behold.*
>
> *Flash Bang Baby, push the spheres.*
> *Yes, no, maybe and I'll be your ears.*
> *Flash Bang Baby, push the skies.*
> *Yes, no, maybe and I'll be your eyes.*
>
> *Warm noise—they come in silent storms*
> *a brave few, who circle round and swarming*
> *our voice—that disappears the normal*

girl–boys, that reeling are transformed.

Flash Bang Baby, push the spheres.
Yes, no, maybe and I'll be your ears.
Flash Bang Baby, push the skies.
Yes, no, maybe and I'll be your eyes.

Anna Z had talked the night before about something she called the Alien Drift. Real aliens? Drifters from The-Far-Out-There? Nobody really believed in such things. The Apollonauts had found nothing but dust and rocks on the moon. And the Mars probe was sending back messages with pretty much the same info. Beings from beyond our solar system? That was all stories for feebs, guesswork and crackpot theories for space-spazzes. Still, there was Django Conn on the stage of the Maxima. There he was on the album covers and inside *Creedo*, looking more like an alien than anybody I'd ever seen. Thin and pale and cold as ether.

TWENTY-SEVEN

"It's not just possible, Davi. It's absolutely real. You were at the show. You saw it and you felt it. You know it and don't try to tell me you don't. The Alien Drift is real, and Django's just a fraction of it, one bright scintilla. You know that word? A scintilla is a spark, or a trace of light, or a gleam. Aliens in the movies might be all gross and disgusting, with big, bulging eyes and sucker-tip tentacles, but that's just to scare the little kiddies. They might come in blasting their death-rays and vaporizing everything they see. Explosions and fighting and big stupido noises. But that's just for show. The moviemakers need something to spend their special effects budget on.

"But the real aliens aren't like that at all. They're the cosmic drifters, the ones who come in like x-rays and pass right through. Nothing can stop them. Nothing can hold them back or push them away. And you know what happens when x-rays go through human flesh? They hit the DNA and scramble it up. You get mutations and that's us.

"They're out there and maybe they always were. I don't know why it's happening now. But it is and you know it deep in your heart and your bones, Davi. You feel it, right?

In your genes and in your DNA. The drift has reached us and they're crossing over. Golden souls from true night, like Django says. Making the transit, a bright wave.

"You said you saw me at the show looking like I'd lost everything. But that's not all of it. There was more, a lot more, going on. Cold light—that's what I was feeling right there at the edge of the stage. Silent storms, pushing the spheres, pushing the skies. It made the others disappear, not me. All the ones who were just there because they thought it was the place to be, or they wanted to be seen and have everybody think they were the Nazz and weren't just normals dressed up like Django.

"I was making the change, Davi. Kneeling and beholding the bright ones. Feeling the wave go through me. And you're next. Your eyes, your ears. Your brain, your heart. And then all of you, Davi, all of you and more.

"Impossible? So what? Django's whole career, all his records, and his whole *life* are impossible. But there he was, right? Live and in person at the Maxima. You saw him and you heard him. What's an Albino Reptile? Does that make sense to you? Where's this Dimension X? Can you explain that to me? Is there such a thing? What in the world does 'Girls Will Be Boys' mean? Django made the wild mutation so why can't we? He was normal once, with a normal name and a family and the whole boring nowhere deal. And now look at him. Now, *listen to him* and tell me he's not impossible."

TWENTY-EIGHT

I thought about sneaking into the middle room again and listening in on Sabina. But I decided instead to go right to her door and knock. As usual, she gave me a disgusted look, as if it pained her just to be reminded that I existed. She stood in the doorway, not even asking me what I wanted, because she knew whatever it was, she wouldn't like it. Her hair was wound into one black cobra-coil and her mascara had the steely gleam of a stiletto blade.

"What was that music yesterday?" I asked, even though I didn't really care about it at all.

She just stood there, glaring at me, lovely and lethal at the same time.

"I heard some music. Was that a harmonium?" Getting no answer out of her, I said I'd seen her friends going down the hall to the elevator. Sabina's answer was the usual, silent, big sister I-can't-stand-you stare.

Carlos was there, too, in Sabina's room. He opened the door the whole way and tried to be a bit friendlier, with his standard fakey, "Hey Davi, what's going on?" He was dressed, as usual, in the best of fashion: expensive fabrics, styled sleekly and perfectly fitted. His hair was black and shiny, and he had a licorice whip mustache. The tips of his lizard-skin boots, and the heels too, had bright bands of silver on them. I guessed he was going for a cosmopolitan cowboy sort of look.

He was playing it cool, pretending that we hadn't seen each other in the hallway the day before. To him, I was a pest, a spy, and a squealer. To me, Carlos was a braggart, a showoff, and some kind of con artist I didn't understand. He even let people think he'd spent time in jail, though I never knew if this was true.

Sabina loved to show him off to her friends, but hate-hate-hated when my path and his crossed. That was easy to explain. I'd broken our deal. I was listening in on them once and found out they were planning to use the honey-moon suite in the west tower for something special and romantic. I never tattletaled to my father, but I let her know what I knew. Carlos thought it was a joke. He didn't care much about getting caught. But Sabina never forgave me for messing up her big night.

"What was that music I heard before?" Of course what I really wanted to ask was "Who was that girl? What can you tell me about her?" Carlos knew why I was there. He'd always been able to see through other people's lies. I suppose liars have to be good at that. He knew why I'd come around now, asking stupido questions.

"Buxtehude's Prelude in A minor," he said, as though overnight he'd become an expert in baroque music.

"We're really busy now," Sabina said, which meant go away and stay away.

"I really need to—"

She cut me off with another "we're busy" and I gave up.

TWENTY-NINE

On the way out of the Angelus, I stopped at the main desk. Armand made one of his little official bows, clicked his shiny heels, and handed me the piece of flimsy, pale green paper. It said just six words: "Meet me at the Tombola. Dusk." It was signed with the letters A and Z.

I asked Armand if the San Panteleone Fair was happening that week. He gave me a smug little nod, as though to say he thought the idea of street fairs and gambling and all-night revelry was a bit embarrassing. Almost no one who stayed at the Angelus would stoop to such common entertainment. Still, a few lowbrow tourists from the New World might ask about it, and as the desk clerk, Armand needed to know everything that was happening in the city. Music, plays, church services, art shows, and even street festivals.

Sabina and I, when we were younger, had played some money away at the Tombola a few times. It was just a big wheel of fortune game at the San Panteleone celebration. There were other amusements too, of course: shooting galleries, ring-toss, knock-the-bottle, Skee-Ball, and lightning lizards. But the Tombola was the center of the fun bazaar and would be easy to find.

I took a side hallway to get a glimpse into my father's office. He was there, in the back, talking with two other men. A shiny, bald head, broad shoulders in a heavy black jacket. I waited a moment, thinking he might look up and give me a smile, or even come out and talk for a little while. But he was busy and didn't notice me there at the door. And even if he'd wanted to talk, what would I tell him? That I knew about the Alien Drift? That the light and the sound from beyond were making me into a mutation?

THIRTY

Dusk was still far away. I had hours to use up before seeing Anna Z again. I thought about going to the fair anyway, to wander around and spend my money and try to burn up the time with not-very-amusing amusements. I was sure, however, that this would just make the wait seem even longer.

So I went to Luigi's record shop, figuring I could poke around in the bins, and maybe soak up a little Anna Z vibe. She'd told me the night before that she used to go to Luigi's, but she'd been staying away lately. When I asked her why, she'd avoided the question, starting in with another of her talk-talk-talking spiels.

The kid from the day before was there again: the one with the wild shag, blue-green jumpsuit, and platforms. This time he was looking through the Django bins, muttering like a street crazy. He wasn't exactly hostile, and he didn't have the strung-out look of a kid on fly-spell. But there was definitely something wrong with him. "Lord of the Fleas, Keeper of the Keys." He turned to look at me. "Kingdom Come, Deaf and Dumb."

"What?" I asked him. "Is that from a song?"

His voice went way up, higher and louder. "Lord of the Fleas!"

Luigi told him to cool it. So he backed away, giving me a sputtery snarl and whispering something about bad vibes. Did he feel something coming off of me, I wondered. Real vibes, radiation, the alien x-rays that were supposedly passing through? Or maybe he was just a little bent in the brain, not a real glister kid but sort of insano, dressing that way in the middle of the day, all by himself.

There was a big poster on the wall, a blown-up version of the cover for the Witch-Babies' new album. It showed an ancient ruined castle. The light was all blurry and throbbing, like one of those infrared shots that show what the naked eye can't see. In the middle, facing the castle, was a pure white man totally naked, holding a pure white little kid above his head like he was giving her up as a sacrifice.

Anna Z hadn't mentioned the Witch-Babies last night. I didn't know if she thought they were part of the mutation too. I was sure, though, that the new album's art pointed in that direction. I went over to the Witch-Babies bin, luckily far from the freak-brain kid, and found there were ten copies of the record. Most of the song titles didn't mean much. But the last cut on the second side was called "Aurora Borealis Uber Alles." I had a blurry idea that the northern lights were some kind of magnetic radiation. Was this connected to the Alien Drift too? I didn't know. But I could buy the album and find out.

THIRTY-ONE

I went from Luigi's shop toward the wharves, thinking that the ripe, salty smell of the sea might clear some of the cobwebs out of my brain. And the sight of the ships that had come from around the world usually made me feel better. Sometimes I'd read the foreign names, watch the sun-blackened sailors at their work, and try to imagine the distant places they'd come from.

That day, everything seemed to shimmer with weird light: purple and sunset-blue, dark crimson and indigo. The granite wharves looked as ancient as the altar on the Witch-Babies' new album cover: gnawed by the salt winds, stained black with oil and the dried slime of a million dead fish. The iron rings in rotted pilings, the curls of greasy smoke, the heave of the waves and the thrumming of engines. It all seemed so wrong, not so much ugly as tainted.

So I fled, back toward San Panteleone. I went past the Archbishop's palace. It never failed—especially that day—to put me in mind of older, far-off times. There was a museum that I'd looked through a few times before. Mostly they had religious vestments, suits of armor, old books, jewelry, relics, and primitive stone carvings. There was, however, a new wing devoted to more modern collections. And they'd just put out for public viewing, I'd heard, one of the moon rocks brought back by the Apollonauts.

THIRTY-TWO

The entrance to the museum had once, many years before, been the doorway that the Archbishop himself had used. Since then they'd rebuilt and rebuilt again, and now there was a little booth where a man in a somber gray suit took money and handed out pamphlets.

I paid, got lost and found and lost again in the winding hallways. Eventually I asked a guard, and he pointed me toward the science and natural history wing. A display of stuffed emperor penguins, standing like soldiers, was first. Then came radios, moviemaking equipment from the New World, lasers and masers and rocket technology. At last, behind tinted glass to keep the light from changing it, was the rock from the moon.

There it sat on its red silk cushion. A rock, that to my eyes, looked no different than any rock I could pick up on the street. About the size of my fist, rough and pitted, it might have been a piece of broken concrete. Seeing the moon rock, so plain, so good for nothing and at the same time priceless, had a strong effect on me. Why was gold so valuable, I wondered. Why did shiny stones like ruby and emerald cost so much when they weren't useful for much? It was about the light, of course, the shine. Silver and gold and bronze. Diamond and sapphire, topaz and carnelian. They all had a gleam or a glister to them, and that was what made them so precious.

The moon rock was dull, with no shine at all. Still, it was more precious than diamonds or platinum because it had traveled across huge expanses of darkness and vacuum. And it had a kind of glow that the naked eye couldn't detect. Infrared or ultraviolet or gamma rays, some form of radiation above or below the range of human sight.

I was in a daze, I suppose, staring at the useless rock and feeling the glow, even though I couldn't see it. That's why, I suppose, I didn't feel the presence of another person entering the room. I didn't know he was there until he'd come up close and aimed those inky black eyes at me.

THIRTY-THREE

He came into the moon rock room, quiet as a shadow. He could be loud, as I later found out, loud as a storm. But right then it was just him and me and the lunar silence. I didn't know his name then, of course, or what he had to do with Anna Z. He'd been following me. That much I could figure out—but why? I didn't know anything about him other than that he could make me feel good-afraid and bad-afraid with just his eyes.

I backed away. He let me have that space for a little while. Still, there was silence in the moon rock room. Soon enough the words would come pouring out. But he knew that silence is just as powerful as noise, or at least it can be if he was the reason for it.

He was dressed mostly in black: jacket, pants, shirt. But his shoes were red. Not girly-red like the Ruby Slippers, but a much deeper, richer shade, like leather made from the skin of a killer squid. I know it doesn't make much sense, but that's where my mind went. I'd seen some pictures of big hungry squid. They were beautiful and horrible at the same time, sleek and grotesque like aliens that lived right here, hidden, on the same planet as me. When they were cranked-up starving, wild to attack and eat, their skin turned that same shade of killer red as those shoes.

That's what I thought of as I looked down at his feet because his eyes were too intense for me to bear. Then he spoke, and I had to look back at his face.

"Why are you here?"

I didn't know how to answer. Because I wasn't sure why I'd come, and why I should tell him even if I knew.

More silence. More afraid. More looking down at his shoes, up at his face.

Then he came closer, very close, and the words oozed out.

THIRTY-FOUR

"I know you know what she knows. Don't bother saying you don't." His voice was liquid. If sounds could be seen with the naked eye, then this would've been a rich indigo, like fine oily dye. Purple-blue with a faint rainbow sheen. "And I know you know where she is right now. I saw her sneaking out of the hotel last night, but she must've known I was watching for her, so she gave me the slip-slip-slide and now she's nowhere to be seen. So the first order of business is for you to tell me where she is."

"I don't know," I said. "I really don't."

He sighed, as though very disappointed. "Here's the way it's got to work. I don't want you to get hurt. You just go with me right now down the hall and out to the street, without making any fuss or getting the guards steamed, and you take me right to where she is. And everything will be fine. Do you think you can do that? Are you okay with that?"

I just stood there, stupido, like he'd hypnotized me.

"She's not going to be your best friend. Trust me on this one. I can save you a lot of grief. A great deal of suffering. You do what I say, and you won't get hurt. Trust me. I know her a hundred times better than you, inside and out, and she's nobody's friend but mine. Never was and never will be. She will lie and cheat and steal and trick you for all you've got and leave you like she thinks she left me. Only I'm not letting her get away with that kind of thing. Not now and not never ever. She's mine, mine, mine. There's no way but *my way*, you understand?"

I nodded, even though I didn't have a clue what he was talking about.

"She's pulled this kind of thing before and it didn't work. So you might as well get it into your brain right now that you're not special, you're not her friend, and she doesn't really want you. She's just winding you round her finger with her lies and her spaced-out talk. What was it this time? No, don't tell me. She gave you the mutation routine—is that it? *Homo lux.* The big alien transformation? Did she tell you all about the creatures of light from the realms of night? Was it angel-talk with you or was it monster movies? No, really, don't tell me. I want to figure this one out all by myself. But in the meantime, you start walking out of the room and down the hall and out of this place. You understand? You do that and you won't have to get hurt."

THIRTY-FIVE

Was he her ex-boyfriend, I asked myself, as we left the moon rock chamber. That had to be it. The way he seemed so jealous—threatened by me even though I had nothing really to threaten him with. Mad, edgy, almost-frantic jealousy: that was the feeling that came off him in waves. She was his in some way I didn't understand, and he would do anything to get her back.

Between the power of Django's glister-sound and Anna Z's alien rants, the invisible lunar rays and now these threats and squidy soft talk, I hardly knew who I was anymore. All my old ways of thinking—true or false, push or pull, freaky or normal—seemed useless. So I did what I was told. I obeyed the voice. "Go. Start walking." I went out, down, and onto the street, in a waking-dreaming daze.

"You don't have any choice. Do you understand? No choice. You've got to tell me where she is." It was like he didn't really want to know, though, because he hardly gave me a second to talk. We went down the block, with him beside me like a bodyguard. Soon the Archbishop's palace was behind us, and we headed into an area where there were far more people on the streets. And more places for them to spend their money: little stores, coffee houses, tourist traps, restaurants, and antique stores.

He went on, "Fate, destiny, call it whatever you want. The hand of the gods. The stars lining up a certain way. The pull of the tides or the magnetic fields. Doesn't matter what you name it. What it means is this: it's going to happen, and it's going to happen only one way. My way. You're in it now, and you're going all the way to the end with me."

He couldn't seem to keep quiet, which was fine with me, because I had no idea where to find Anna Z, even if I was willing to squeal on her. No question, if and when he got a hold of her, things would get pretty bad. He seemed to love her and hate her at the same time. So I let him talk and tried to clear my head enough to make a plan.

THIRTY-SIX

"Did she do her Alien Freak Show routine? She always does. Did she tell you she was all stitched together, scar tissue, wires and bolts inside, hunks of this body and chunks of that one? 'Everybody loves the freak show.' Right? Did she say that too? 'They all want to know where the real me ends and the fake me begins. Is there anything left? Not much, just the voice, half my brain, the left eye, some of the spine, the right hand, and some guts. The rest is fake, spare parts stolen from corpses.'" His voice changed as he imitated Anna Z, getting high and quavery. It didn't sound anything like her, at least not the way she'd talked to me.

"Dead or alive, fate or dumb luck, one way or the other, you're in it with me. And you're not getting out until I have Anna Z back. That's all I want. That's all I need. You understand? And then nobody gets hurt. I'm actually doing you a huge favor. I know how she gets, with all those stories. I know what it feels like. But trust me on this. You have no idea what kind of grief I'm saving you from.

"That's right. Saving. You're dead if you don't do it my way. But if you do, you're saved. From me, and from her, and from everything she'll drag you into."

My father had said we should have guards to keep us safe. Once in a while the kids of businessmen did get grabbed for ransom. I heard about a girl—her father owned one of the big shipping lines—who got snatched and sold back for a fortune. Once we'd gotten rid of our last tutor though, Sabina said that she was an adult and there was no way she'd put up with a paid goon following her around. And my silhouette was so small I always doubted any kidnappers even knew I existed. Still, here I was being marched down the street like a prisoner going to the scaffold to be hanged.

THIRTY-SEVEN

"Listen close. She's no man-made monster. I know her better than anybody in the world. She's the real thing. She speaks with forked tongue, but it's still her tongue, the one she was born with. There's not a single part of her body that's fake. Not even a filling in a tooth or a press-on fingernail. She's never even dyed her hair. It's all real—top to bottom, inside and out. I know this for sure like nobody else. She's a hundred percent authentic all herself."

Of course I had to escape from him. Every minute that passed got me closer to something horrible. That much was for sure. I don't think he really wanted to kill me, at least not that day. Later, though, once he had Anna Z back and didn't need me. Then he'd squash me like a stinkbug. But that day, he was still trying to find out what was what and how much I really knew. He gave me lot of pretty crazy threats, but obviously I had something he wanted. So as we marched down the canal side, over the Bridge of Tears toward the Hessian Quarter, I was running a dozen different plans.

None of them, as it turned out, would've worked. Too clever, too much like spies and secret agents. I could eavesdrop at the Angelus. I could disappear there like a ghost. But this was out in the street. And my captor was bigger than me, way stronger too, and dead set on getting me to a place where he could squeeze the truth out, like juice from a blood orange. I could try tricks and ruses, but I knew that I didn't have what it takes.

So my body took over: I just started screaming. It was that simple. My brain wasn't working very well so my body took over. A hundred people were passing us by. Another thousand were on the streets all around us. There was no way he'd kill me right there in public. And as soon as the screaming started, he got very freaked out.

"Shut up!" he growled. "Shut your mouth!"

I screamed louder. He started shouting back. Seeing how it was working, my brain clicked on, and I turned up the volume even more. That put even more panic into him, with me wailing away right there in the middle of the San Gregorio plaza. People stared, of course. Some tourists pulled out their cameras. And a little rat-faced lady started yelling for the Guardia to come and get rid of us.

That was all it took. He might be able to make me do whatever he wanted. But he couldn't stand up to a Guardia patrol with their handcuffs and shock rods. So he let me go. Spitting out threats about coming after me later, he headed off across the bridge and into the crowd on the far side of the canal. People gaped at me, though not for very long. Free, and safe for the time being, I shut up and headed as fast as my shaking legs would go toward San Panteleone.

THIRTY-EIGHT

There was still some sunlight in the sky. The moon was already up though, a thin pale ghost rising over the eastern skyline. With the darkness gathering and the cool of evening, I calmed down a little. My heart finally slowed to normal as I heard the far-off rumbling of drums. San Panteleone was famous for its music: peasant folk groups from the old days, jazzy dance bands, fiddlers and panpipers and, for the kids, loud basement clubs around the edges of the fair. I wasn't quite close enough to tell what kind of music it was floating through the streets. Most likely it was a blend, with the motors of the rides thrumming in time with the dance tunes and shadow-marches.

I was still carrying the album from Luigi's. The fear-sweat from my hand had soaked the bag along the bottom. I shifted it a quarter turn and held the flat package to my chest, like an amulet to keep me safe. So far it had worked, and I wasn't about to change my luck. The Witch-Babies and their Ancient Altar would go with me throughout the entire night.

Closer to the fair, the strands of sound pulled themselves apart. I could tell now the squeal of girls on the

Wizard Wheel from the squeal of a reed-pipe. The booming rhythms were both mechanical and musical. A band organ played its maniacal tunes, as loud as any amplified barytons or gambas. The sound was relentless, hundreds of pipes wailing in complex fugues and rondos. And nearer to the fair, I could tell the difference between firecrackers and bursting balloons.

THIRTY-NINE

There was no charge to enter the fair, though a price was attached to everything else. Visitors could get a peek at Doctor Contorto, knotting his limbs like pieces of rope. But if they wanted to see his most amazing stunts, they had to lay down a little cash. A nautch dancer from India did her slinky routine. The best parts of the show—more skin and the snakiest moves—were only to be seen inside her canvas-sided booth. The joyrides lurched with lights flashing, and the bumper-cars bashed and smashed. To have the real fun, to feel the spin and the bang, people had to pay. I could have done that. I never was without enough money. And a week earlier, before meeting Anna Z, I might've. But I'd come for only one reason, to find her, and fun-rides didn't seem very fun that night. Still, the familiar scents, as I went deeper into the fair, had a reassuring effect on me. Roasted garlic, burned out Roman candles, steamy pesto bread, spilled red wine, ouzo, and cauldrons of scalding olive oil.

Named after one of the city's patron-saints, the fair was supposedly a religious event. And a person could buy holy water bottled at far-off Fatima, Knock, and Lourdes. There were Virgin Mary dolls wrapped in cellophane, plaster icons, and booths filled with sacred heart medallions. These had their place, which got farther and farther from the fun with each passing year.

The center of the fair was the great Tombola. I went straight there, or as straight as I could in such a heavy-duty crowd. I bought ten tickets to gamble and edged my way up to the front. The wheel spun. People yelled and moaned and whimpered as it slowed. A man with a megaphone and a voice like a poison toad called out to close the betting.

A big cheer and a bigger groan greeted the winning number. I pushed more tickets onto the board. The wheel spun again, and I felt a hand on my shoulder. People were shoving and yanking so I didn't pay it much mind. Then I felt warm breath in my ear and turned to see Anna Z gazing at me.

As soon as I saw her I tossed away my tickets and started jabbering. "There was a guy. He's looking for you. He said he'd kill me. I think he was serious."

She told me to be quiet, though in the press of frantic gamblers I doubt anyone could've heard anything we said. Taking my hand, she led me out of the crowd to an alleyway between booths where we could talk. She leaned with me into the shadow, and her voice fell to a whisper.

FORTY

"Okay, okay, just calm down a little and listen. I'll tell you the whole thing but you've got to listen and not interrupt. Just let me talk, and then we'll figure out a plan. He really is serious business, serious as brain surgery. So we have to get this right. I didn't think he'd find me so fast, but he did and now we don't have a lot of time."

"But who is he?"

"His name is Lukas."

"I don't understand. Why is he so—"

"Just let me talk. I saw the whole thing on the plaza. You and my brother. Wait, wait, don't say anything. Let me explain. Yes, he's my brother. His name is Lukas. I knew he wouldn't do anything drastic right there in public, so I was waiting for the right time. Then you started in screaming, which was pretty wild and exactly the right move. I didn't expect you to melt down like that, but Lukas can't stand that kind of thing. He gets very freaked when he's not in control. It won't work again. He'll have a better plan to shut you up. But it worked just fine then. So I followed you here, and we've got tonight to get it right."

"He's really your brother? I thought he wanted to kill

you. Or me. Or both of us." My thoughts were getting ahead of my tongue. "Why does he hate me so much? What did I do?"

"Listen to me, Davi, I ran away from home. From him, my brother Lukas. It feels like about a year to me, or a whole lifetime, since we saw Django. That was the day I ran away. And that's the whole reason this is all happening. All he wants is me, back again. Me back home, the two of us like it's been forever. Me and thee, he and she. Sister and brother and no other."

"Is that from a song?" I was shaking, the confusion filling my whole body. "What are you talking about?"

"You can say goodbye right now, if all this is too freaky, and you don't want to get mixed up any more. You can say it and I'll be all right. I'll keep running by myself. But that's not what I want. It's time for me to be free. Gone, gone, maximum gone. Just like Django said, remember? 'Push the spheres. Push the skies. I'll be your ears. I'll be your eyes.' What I want is to be free, us together, you and me."

FORTY-ONE

Of course there were a lot of things I liked about Anna Z: the look on her face when she was deep into music, the look of her body when she was lying on my bed, the feel of her breath in my ear when she was whispering secrets, the way she turned toward me, instead of away like most people. But there was no question, the thing I liked most, or even *loved*, was the sound of her voice and the feel of her words going into me.

Some of the time it was just gibberish. Or a mix of song lyrics, folkie-tales, truth, and whatever came buzzing through her head. She liked the sound of her voice too, and the fact that I'd listen without telling her that she wasn't making much sense. That night, leaning together in the shadows, with the sounds of the fair storming around us, I listened and I loved it. I also knew that I had to find out what was really going on. Beautiful, wild gibberish is great, but Lukas was no overcooked fantasy. He looked dead serious when he said I would surely die if I didn't tell him where to find Anna Z.

I listened some. I let her roll for a while. Then when she slowed down to take a breath, I said, "Stop. Okay?

Just stop for a second. I need to know what's going on. Everything."

She took my hand, like we were standing on the edge of a huge cliff and she was afraid she'd jump off if I didn't hold her back. "It's bad. It's real bad."

"Tell me. Just say it."

She started in again with another spiel of words, and I told her again to stop it. I had to know what was true or Lukas was going to tear me, and maybe her also, to pieces. She began one more time. I ended it again. She gave me a long, sad sigh, as though I'd closed up her favorite game. Light from rides was flashing on the lens of her glasses, so I couldn't see her eyes.

She let loose another of her heartbreaking sighs then gave me the facts. The sound of her voice changed, the pressure and the speed fell as she talked.

"Lukas is really my big brother. I ran away from home again. The first time, he found me within twenty-four hours and locked me down for a month. He needs to be in control. He's the king and I'm the queen, but you know, queens don't have any say over what happens to them. That's the way it's always been between us. The second time, last year during the moon landing, I managed to stay away for a week. Then he tracked me to an abandoned building that kids were using for a squat. Two of those kids ended up in the hospital with broken arms. Jules, the kid who organized the squat, nobody saw him again. This is my third time on the run, and if he catches me now, I don't think I can survive it. This is for real, Davi. I don't think I'll make it if he finds me."

FORTY-TWO

My first idea was to talk to the Guardia. It had to be against the law to hold a girl prisoner like her brother did. "That won't work," she said. "I already tried it. I'm underage, and Lukas is my legal guardian. He knows how to play the courts and judges."

"I have money," I told her. "I can hire a lawyer. My father knows some of the best in the city." She shook her head, sadder than before. Law was useless.

She put her arms around me and started crying. For a second, I thought this was just more show, a new routine she hadn't used on me yet. But if it was fake, she was the best actress in the world. Tears: real. The weakness in her body: real. A change in her voice too. The words came now even quieter and more unsure.

"We've been together, the two of us, since we were little. Our parents died from some kind of plague that the sailors brought from Egypt." This sounded a little made-up, but I didn't press her on it. "We had a foster mother for a while. Sweet Jesu, she was awful. Mean and stupido and she didn't care about us at all. We called her the Wicked Witch of the Yeast because she ran a bakery shop. Then

Lukas figured out a plan of escape and we did it." This too sounded kind of vague and made-up. "He got a hold of some of the family money, and we moved together to a place in the Hessian quarter, out beyond the Black Lagoon, where we've been ever since."

I asked her if I could buy Lukas off maybe, pay some kind of ransom. I was sure I could get plenty of cash. This made her furious, and she pulled away, snuffling and wiping at her face like the tears were poison. She turned her back to me and jerked free when I tried to touch her.

FORTY-THREE

"How can you talk like that? Haven't you been listening to anything I was saying? He's been treating me like he owned me since I was little, since before I can remember. And now you want to buy me like I'm a slave or a pet or something? Nobody owns me! Understand? I need help. I need a friend, and I thought you were the one."

"I am. But I just want to—"

"The guy I ran off with the first time was perfect slime. He promised me all sorts of nice things and said he'd protect me. He claimed he had a place where I could stay and be safe. But when it came down to it, money talked, and he took a handful of cash and called Lukas and that was that. You understand, Davi? He wanted to make me into something that could be bought and sold, and Lukas was willing to pay the most. So Mr. Slime just got rid of me and went looking for another girl to sell.

"When I ran away the second time, I had a better shot at it. The kids at the squat were okay for a while. I thought I'd be safe there, and for a while I was. But one of them squealed me in to my brother. The kid was doing way too much white gong and wanted some easy money. So he sold me! You understand, Davi? One of the kids where I'd gone to escape and be safe sold me back to my brother for money. Some of them tried to help. But I told you, Lukas broke them up like little sticks and threw them away. And Jules, he was the one I liked the most there, ended up vanished. Into the North Canal, I think.

"So don't ever talk about buying or selling me ever again. Money isn't going to help. It only makes things worse. It always does. Money is dirt and dirt makes things dirty. There's no way around that. So be my friend, Davi. Help me figure out a plan to get away and stay away. Safe, forever. Can you do that? Be my friend. I really need a friend now, Davi. And you're all I've got."

FORTY-FOUR

It was impossible for me to say no to that.

"Of course I'll help you," I said, though I had almost nothing to offer. "We'll figure it out. We'll make a good plan."

What did I have that would be of any use? Stacks of records, piles of fan mags, posters on my walls. Those would keep her safe for about a half second if her brother showed up at my room. Asking Sabina for help might be okay, but I didn't trust Carlos and hardly knew the rest of her friends. That left me with myself: who I was and what I knew. And besides music, what I knew best was the Angelus.

I'd been sneaking around there since I could walk. I knew it better than anybody, even the hotel detectives my father had to keep things running smoothly. I knew it better than the cleaning people and room service waiters because they had their special areas and I could go anywhere. The plumbers and electricians had access to the tunnels and the attics and closed-off corridors. But they never sat in the main lobby, watching the guests come and go, or went backstage to see the tango dancing in the fifth floor ballroom.

What I had to offer was the Angelus, which would be safe for Anna Z for a long time. Maybe forever. There were rooms where no one, absolutely no one, ever went. I got food for myself whenever I wanted. The cooks and serving maids wouldn't ask any questions if I took a little more. And best of all, her brother couldn't just wander around the halls all day. No matter how well he dressed, Lukas wouldn't pass for very long as a normal guest at the hotel.

I explained this all to Anna Z, still standing in the shadows at the fair. Girls screamed as the rides spun them through the air. Boys yelled, some drunk and some pretending to be drunk. Drums and trumpets from a marching troupe echoed all around us. Anna Z asked me if I'd really do that for her, really take her to the Angelus and give her a safe place. When I'd said "yes" for the third time, she put her arms around me, strong and tight, and put her lips on mine. This was the first real kiss I'd ever had. I didn't drink wine or do fly-spell, but I knew then what they felt like. And buzzed that way, I headed with Anna Z back to the Angelus.

FORTY-FIVE

It took a long time because we avoided every street and bridge where the lamps burned brightly. A torchlight procession of acolytes came chanting from San Panteleone, and we had to detour far around their path. People spilled from the doors of taverns and nightclubs. Two members of the Guardia came walking toward us at one point, and we hurried down a totally unlit alleyway. All this moving from darkness to darkness added to the sense that we were going to a place unknown. Yes, of course I understood the ins and outs of the Angelus better than anyone. Still, with Anna Z there, the entire hotel would have a new and unknown feel.

Reaching the hotel from the walkway along the canal, we went down a narrow backstreet and slipped in through the cook-and-baker's entry. Only one old man might have seen us come in, and I think he was asleep. Taking Anna Z's hand, I led her quickly through a low passage and down two flights of stone stairs.

Once, when Sabina and I had escaped from our tutor—a vicious little crow of a woman, with black, pinprick eyes—we spent an entire day hiding in this part of the hotel. We came back at supper time, filthy with cobwebs and coal dust. Our tutor made life for us even worse after that, until we made up some outrageous lies to tell our father. Maria-Claire vouched for us and that got the tutor fired. For the time being, this set of layered basements was where Anna Z would have to stay.

I took her to one of my secret hideouts. It had been a while since I'd spent any time there. Still, it would be fine until I prepared a better place. There was a couch, a few broken-down chairs, a fridge that didn't work, and a pile of books from my pirate phase. A few years back, before I moved on to the Witch-Babies, the Starry Crowns, V-Rocket, and then Django, I'd spent all my time reading about Moorish pirates. I even got some clothes together to make a costume, though I never once wore it where anybody would see.

The hideout had no windows, and the steam pipes weren't hooked up so it might get cold. But the lights came on. There were some blankets on the couch and a little electric heater I'd brought in when this was one of my winter hideouts. I showed her down the hall to a bathroom that luckily still had running water. I told her I'd go get some food. Anna Z thanked me with words and another kiss. I went off a different way than we'd come, working my way in a maze-loop to the lower kitchen.

FORTY-SIX

When I finally got back to my room, the sun was just coming up. I stood at the east window and looked out at the city. I was exhausted of course, having been up all night. Almost getting killed by Lukas, going to the fair, Anna Z's trippy spieling and sneaking through the back streets with her. All of those had seriously messed with my mind. It didn't explain, though, what I saw—or thought I saw.

The Alien Drift was real. That's what hit me as I gazed out at the sunlight growing, glowing behind the tops of buildings. What I saw looked like spirit-bodies floating in the sky. Or bombs made of misty light, dropped from unseen, unheard zeppelins, drifting slowly down on the city. Or human spears thrown from heaven.

The sky that morning looked like a thin foil of hammer-beaten metal. What I saw was the cosmic drifters, the living x-rays, passing through and making that shimmering metallic light. They were real, crossing over. Gold and silver souls making the bright wave.

Rays and waves made the whole of the invasion from beyond. Aliens aren't bug-eyed space-things. They're not just actors in rubber masks or dwarves with cheap makeup and funny clothes. There aren't any talking dragons from Alpha Centuri or little green men. I could forget about flying saucers and The Mole-boys from Mars. The big-eyed, bigheaded aliens aren't any more realistic than a fairy godmother. It's about energy, light and sound, and that's all. People make aliens into two-legged humanoids with heads and hands, or blubbery slug creatures, because it's too hard to deal with the truth. It's all radiation passing through us. Light and sound making movies in our heads. And that's all.

FORTY-SEVEN

Waking up, I heard the bells of St. Florian's. *That* was normal. Feeling hungry and stiff was normal too. Then it all came flooding back, and I turned my head to look out the window. The metallic light was gone. The human sky-shapes had passed. It might've been any other day of my life. Except Anna Z was downstairs, far below, and I had a job to do now—keeping her free and safe from her brother.

I surprised myself by not going straight to the subbasement. Maybe I was afraid that she'd taken off already, changed her mind about trusting me and fled. So I did what I needed to do.

First I cleaned myself up a little. Hair, teeth, clothes. Then I went to Hermann, the head of the hotel detectives and told him a lie about Lukas. Hermann was a big man, always in a shabby suit and smelling of old coffee and stale bay rum. He listened as I explained that there was a scary guy Sabina had invited to one of her séances. Hermann knew about the comings and goings of her spiritualist friends and didn't like any of them. This guy, though, I told him, was not just a fool and a fake, but a real criminal who'd threatened my sister. She wouldn't let Hermann know any of this, because she didn't want our father to get upset and shut down the séances. But I'd seen the whole mess, I told Hermann, and this guy really shouldn't be let into the Angelus, ever. He believed me, and he actually thanked me. He took a description of Anna Z's brother and said he'd make sure he didn't make any trouble.

Next I went up to the northwest tower to see if my other old hideout room was still good. This one was the total opposite of the one in the basement. Bright and big, with windows facing three directions, it was a suite that many guests would've loved to stay in. My father had closed it up, however, years before. And no one was allowed up there. Even when we were sneaking around together, Sabina refused to go to the suite.

I used my set of passkeys, got into the tower stairway and climbed two flights of red-carpeted steps. I opened up the suite, and other than the musty smell and the fine layer of dust, it was perfect.

FORTY-EIGHT

Usually I grabbed something in the east kitchen. Fabian, the main chef there, always treated me right. And the waitresses who'd been working at the Angelus since before I was born took care of me too. They'd make me up a plate of pasta or cold roast pork or garlic bread and red olives and cheese. I'd eat at one of the tables for the staff or take my food to one of the back offices if I felt like being alone.

Now, with a box of food made up for me by Maria-Claire, a carafe of coffee, and even a new fan mag I got from the hotel news dealer, I went down to Anna Z's hiding place. I was nervous as I fiddled the key into the door. I didn't think the whole night before had been a dream, and I was about to wake up. I just wasn't sure if she'd stayed.

A little spasma of panic went through me. The couch was empty. I whispered her name, though shouting it wouldn't have made us any less safe. The lights were on, and I saw a complex pattern of footprints on the dusty floor. I said her name a little louder now, and she peeked out from the closet. I asked if she was okay and she nodded. Setting down the box and the carafe, I went over and took both her hands in mine.

First thing, I described to her what I'd seen in the sky. She said it was electrum light and that she'd seen it before. "Electrum is an alloy, a mix of silver and gold."

It was clear she didn't have a million words in her that afternoon, so I didn't dig deeper, though of course I would have to soon enough. We drank coffee, ate sweet rolls and prosciutto and cheese. Actually, she did most of the eating, making me wonder when her last meal had been.

When she'd gathered up the last crumbs on her fingertips and licked them clean, she wanted to know what was next. I told her I had a better hideout for her, safer because absolutely nobody ever went there. Of course she asked why this place was so different than all the other suites. "I'll explain later," I said. "Right now, we need to get up there without being seen."

FORTY-NINE

This was a lot harder than just me going to the suite. The cooks and maids, the detectives and lobby staff were so used to seeing me wander the Angelus, it was like I was invisible. Anna Z was a different story. I thought about dressing her in a disguise, maybe a wig from the hairdresser's shop and some of Sabina's clothes. This would be too big of a production though. I thought about waiting until well past midnight when the hallways and elevators were mostly empty. And this seemed not a bad idea. What we came up with though was much simpler: I took a maid's uniform from the laundry, grabbed a cleaning cart loaded with sheets and towels, and Anna Z passed through the hotel totally unnoticed. She was the right age to be a maid, and with slumped shoulders and mop bucket, it was like no one could see her.

With a little map I drew for her, she went off on her own. Fifteen minutes later, we met up at a stairway in the northwest tower.

"Nobody noticed you?" I asked.

She shrugged, still pretending to be a downtrodden chambermaid. "I don't think so."

"I'll get rid of the cart," I said.

Anna Z told me to turn around and quickly shucked off the baggy dress. I heard the slink of cloth pulled over her legs and the clunk of shoes tossed to the side. "Okay. You can turn back now." She was herself again. After undoing the braid and shaking out her hair, she took a long breath and let it go slowly, blowing out the last of her nervousness.

Four flights up then silently along the hall, we went hand in hand. I let go to pull out my passkeys, and we slipped inside the suite. Anna Z went straight to the window and looked out at the city. From that height and angle, it was beautiful, the best view in the entire hotel. The spires of St. Florian's stood up like wands made of silver and gold, or electrum as Anna Z called it. The Duce's Dome was far off, but gleamed and glittered in the afternoon sun. Two canals lay before us, slim black serpentine rivers crawling toward the sea.

She asked, of course, why this suite was never used. I told her, in as few words as possible. "This was where my family used to live. Sabina remembers it a little, or at least she claims to. I was born there, in the bedroom, supposedly. My mother died a week later. And my father moved us out, closed the suite up, and we've never been back." Because I had no memory of being there, or knowing my mother, it called up no bad feelings for me. "When I need to be by myself this is always the place to go. It's safe here, and secret, and I can really be alone."

FIFTY

So we got past that for the time being. She understood that I didn't want to say any more about my family, just like she didn't want to explain any more then about her brother. I'd figured out a good plan, we'd made it happen, and she was safe in the suite.

I went back down to the maid's storeroom in my wing to get together clean towels and a toothbrush and some shampoo. Then I stopped in my room to grab a few books for Anna Z to read until I'd hooked up a stereo with headphones. Passing Sabina's door, I heard a murmur of voices. I knocked and she asked who it was.

"It's me, Davi. Come on, open up. I need to talk."

"Go away," she said, annoyed as usual. "And stay away."

I knocked again, making it plain I wasn't leaving until we'd talked. Carlos opened the door and gave me a look that was half-amused and half-menace. "What's so important?" he asked. "Did you buy a new teeny-mag? Or do you have some cool pictures you need to show off?"

I was stubborn, or maybe a little braver that day, taking his sneers and dismissive digs. So after a while, my sister gave up and said I could come in for a few minutes. I got right to the reason for my visit. "How do you know Anna Z?"

"Who?" She poured about a gallon of contempt over that one small word.

"The girl who was here yesterday. The one with the glasses and all that hair. What do you know about her?"

Sabina looked over at Carlos, and he looked away. "She's trash, coming around here where she doesn't belong." They had met her, as she'd told me, at Santa Lucia's. They'd talked mostly about people they knew, places they'd been. Then they'd gotten into the séances, and Anna Z wanted to know all about them.

Carlos didn't say a word about Anna Z. He fiddled with one of my sister's candles, lighting it, blowing it out, relighting it. This silence struck me as odd. He always took the lead, and here he was letting Sabina do all the talking.

She wrinkled up her nose, as though Anna Z was a poor farmer's daughter who smelled of pigs. Then, with one of her nasty little laughs, she told me how impressed Anna Z had been with the hotel. Apparently, Sabina thought it was funny that somebody without much money, who'd done almost no traveling, could look down on their so-called High Necromantic Rites.

I didn't care about that at all. Trying to talk to the dead seemed a big fake, the kind of thing young kids did to scare themselves at sleep-over parties. Sabina was older than me, but right then, I felt like the grown-up, interested in something a lot more serious than ghosts and Ouija boards.

I got up my nerve and asked, "Do you know somebody called Lukas? He's about your age, and I think there's something wrong with him in the head. Very weird. Very intense." I described his look. Both of them seemed uneasy, not exactly afraid, but definitely in no mood to say any more. I asked them again. They both lied—I'm sure of that—telling me that they had no idea who or what I was talking about. Before I could press any harder, Carlos showed me to the door. Sabina went back to poking around in her tea leaves.

FIFTY-ONE

I read in the evening paper that they'd be showing *Frankenstein at the End of Time* on the late show. We needed to see it, together. I was positive of that. It was a sign: they were showing an Apollonautic monster movie at midnight on our first full day together. So I snuck a small TV out of a room the maintenance guys had set up as a lounge. They'd complain to each other, but not to anyone above them. They'd taken the TV and weren't about to protest their stolen goods being stolen.

A little before midnight, with a big plate of anise cakes I snagged from the kitchen, we wrapped ourselves in blankets to keep warm and sat down to see the show. It was a story that had the creature and the doctor, but in the world they moved through, there were no Gothic towers or craggy mountain peaks. This was more like a moonscape, with colonists in high-tech bubble cities. Beyond the bubble the world was empty, cold, and barren.

The best sequence was with the creature escaping from the bubble, out into the empty nowhere-land and the doctor following. The creature either needed no air or could breathe the vacuum. And with the lower gravity, he moved graceful as a dancer. The doctor had to wear a special suit, with a glass dome helmet and clunky boots. So as the doctor chased after the creature, it was like they'd been reversed. The one who was supposed to be a man looked like a clumsy monster, and the one who'd been monstrous glided across the moonscape like a beautiful vapor-trail ghost.

After it was over, we sat there a long time, looking out at the city: brightness and blackness perfectly combined. The Duce's Dome might've been where travelers to this world had landed and set up their base. A spire beyond glowed in cool, pearly light. It was the great steeple on Our Lady, The Queen of Heaven. But it stood up like a rocket ship readying for takeoff.

FIFTY-TWO

"So what did you think?" I asked her.

"It was okay. But I like the early ones better. Black and white—very cool. Shades of silver—nothing looks better. Did you ever see *Bride of Frankenstein*? That's my fave. Elsa Lanchester was the bride, and she plays Mary Shelly, the writer, too. A double role. And did you ever think that Django was like Frankenstein? I mean the doctor and the creature, both of them at the same time. He found the lost manuscripts and did the secret experiments, and he made himself into something new. Django made himself, you understand?"

"Not really," I said, feeling a buzz and a blur in my head.

"He's the creator and the creature at the same time. He took some of this and some of that, stole some riffs, and copied some moves. And once in an interview, he claimed that he was a genius because he let himself get zapped by lightning at midnight. In an abandoned graveyard. Naked."

"He said a lot of things. I read in a story by T.V. Geist that he—"

Anna Z cut off me. The words were coming stronger now, like a train building up steam, picking up speed. "He created himself and came up with another name. Then he let it loose, the brand new sound, just like the Bride of Frankenstein's first scream. There's nothing wilder or sexier in the whole world than her, than Elsa Lanchester in that movie, screaming with the white lightning-bolt in her beehive hairdo. It's like Tarzan's wild-man yodeling in the movies. You think that's just one guy making all that sound? No, that's a Frankenstein yell. It's a lion roaring played backward, and steam whistles blasting in slo-mo, and the scream of the west wind on New Year's Eve, all mixed together like body parts to make a monster.

"Sometimes, I think Mary Shelley's the really amazing one. Not Frankenstein himself or the creature. Can you believe that she was only seventeen when she ran off with a famous poet, who was already married, and wrote the book? No job. No real money. No family. Do you have any idea what people thought about her for doing that, going away with him? But she did it, and they went to the mountains to be free, and that's where she wrote *Frankenstein*. The book was written by a girl. That's what everybody forgets. A teenager. Not some old hag-lady, but a girl the same age as me.

"I read *Frankenstein* about a hundred times, looking for the good parts, piecing together the secrets, digging into the lost world where I knew the truth could be found. It's mostly overheated feelings, more romance than gore and gross-out. There's loving and loathing and losing. The words are stiff sometimes, way too big and complicated. 'To examine the causes of life, we must first have recourse to death.' That kind of thing. 'Do you share my madness?'

Dr. Frankenstein says all sorts of stuff like that. So the story is mostly hidden between the lines. I had to look close to see the real story. Lightning and body parts, ugliness and lust, a killer creature, ice fields in the far north. That's all in there. I got that, but I knew there had to be more. And I was right."

FIFTY-THREE

Then she was quiet. That late, the city and the hotel too were hushed. We sat together a long time, saying nothing. The moon was reflected in her glasses, two smears of pale white light.

"Loving and loathing and losing," she'd said. "Do you share my madness?" Were those just pretty words from a book or something that was true and really mattered? How would I ever know? I loved to listen. When she talked it was like walls and curtains and veils fell, and I could see what was real behind them. As soon as the words stopped, though, everything was hidden again.

The silence flowed in, and what I was sure of, again, was danger, somewhere beyond my sight. Django might be telling us amazing secrets. The Alien Drift might really slide through me like sunbeams through glass. But Anna Z's brother was still out there in the city. Lukas was real flesh and blood. He knew who I was and where I lived. And he wanted Anna Z back.

I said maybe I should stay with her that night. She shook her head and said, "That wouldn't be a good idea. I'll be fine." The door locks were solid. Nobody had a clue that she up was there anyway. And she was right: it would be better to keep things normal. If anyone noticed I hadn't been in my room, like Sabina or one of the maids, they might wonder what was going on and start asking questions. This made sense. Until we had a better plan, I should act as though nothing had changed.

FIFTY-FOUR

Except, of course, everything *had* changed. When I got back to my room, I found Carlos there, smoking in the darkness. The end of his cigarette pulsed, almost died, then pulsed again back to brightness. The moon's milky glimmer stretched across the carpeted floor. I shut the door and said, "What are you doing here? What do you want?"

Away from Sabina, he was different. The way he spoke, the way he looked at me and pushed questions at me were all colored by a feeling of threat. He started talking about my sister and me. He called her "Sabby," which sounded wrong, and he called me "Little Davi," making my name into a sneer. A match broke into sudden flame, and another cigarette began to glow. "You two are spoiled brats, with no idea how the real world works." Poking the bright orange ember at me, he said, "You're messing with people who can make life really hard."

He lit another match and tossed it at me. The little flame died in midair. "Your friend Lukas came around tonight. I was down at The Red Angel. Sabby hates that place. Too many low-lifes for her. I go there by myself. And Lukas found me. He's not in a good mood, and he has a lot to say. He thinks you know where his sister is."

He smoked in silence for a while, letting those last words hang in the air. Then he said, "I lied a little bit earlier. I didn't want Sabby getting worried. Of course I know Lukas. If you run with a certain crowd, you can't help but know him. You were right. He's very intense. And there is something wrong with him in the head. He's got very peculiar ideas about his sister. And he thinks you're up to no good. Spending a little too much time with her. Doing things you shouldn't be doing."

Carlos leaned toward me, and I saw a faint glimmer of a smile. "I can see why you like Anna Z. I like her too, a lot. I wouldn't mind if she—"

"Shut up," I told him. "Just stop talking about her, okay?" The thought of Carlos sleazing up to Anna Z made me sick.

"Fine. Fine. We don't need to say any more about her. You understand what I'm talking about. So what's it going to be, Davi?"

"What do you mean?"

"I can get on the phone right now and have a little talk with Lukas. I can tell him you've been asking the wrong kind of questions about the wrong girl. So what's it going to be? A big complicated mess or a simple transfer of funds? Meeting up with Lukas again or moving a little cash my way?" He said how much he wanted, and he told me exactly how to get the money to him without anyone else, especially Sabina, knowing about it. I didn't argue. There wasn't any point.

FIFTY-FIVE

After he'd left, I went to stand in the wash of moonglow. I could feel it. I know it's not possible, but I could feel the rays reflecting off the moon and down to where I stood. Two hundred thousand miles across emptiness, from the moon's cold surface to me, through the windowpanes, and onto my bare face and arms. I felt it the way I've felt wind on my skin. Cool and smooth as a breeze. I was a secret citizen now of Radiation Nation. Just like Django put it in the song. Just like Anna Z said it to me. I was glowing, right there in my room, glowing pale, lunar white. I took off my shirt and my pants and everything and stood there a long time, soaking up the rays and giving them back, just like the moon.

What else could I do? That's what I asked myself, and there was no good answer. Call my father and tell him everything? That truly was impossible. I couldn't say the words and he couldn't hear them. Talk to Hermann, maybe offer him some money on the side to get his men together and take care of Lukas once and for all? That wasn't an absurd idea. He'd cleaned up messes before. I doubted, though, that he'd be willing to risk his position by breaking the law that way for me. Should I contact the Guardia? Or even the Archbishop's people? None of these would work. So instead, I went to the light.

Of course, I should have been freaking out. Or at least moving quickly to fight back against Carlos and Anna Z's brother. And I suppose part of me was in panic. In my mind somewhere, a voice shouted at me to Do Something! Move, Make a Plan, Counterattack! A much stronger voice said that I was already doing exactly the right thing.

Standing in the light. *Being* the light. *Homo lux*, bright stars like Django Conn and the Albino Reptiles from Dimension X. Like V-Rocket and the Witch-Babies. That was us, Anna Z and me. We had what almost no one could even imagine. We got the music—the sound and light—the way only a few other silver-golden souls could get it. And so there had to be another way, our way, to get free and stay that way.

FIFTY-SIX

The next day, I asked her straight up, "What exactly does your brother want from you? Why is getting you back so important?" Sure, I understood about brothers and their sister. Genes and protoplasm, family lines, growing up together, having things in common that nobody else in the whole world could share. "I have a sister. I get it, chromosomes are forever." But she hated her brother. Or at least she feared him all the way to hate. She'd run away three times. She'd sworn that she could never go back.

I was ready to put everything I had into making this happen. It was like I was living in two worlds, though. There was one where the real hardcore danger moved around in the shadows: thug-brothers and blackmailing slimes like Carlos. In the other world, the real things were sky vapor, bodiless voices, ethereal light and sound. I had to live and do what was needed in both worlds. That was clear to me now, eating with Anna Z up in the secret suite. Scrambled eggs, fresh black bread, and oranges to fill up our stomachs. Sweet coffee that went right to my head: strong caffeine and sugar.

Why, I needed to know, was Lukas so dead set on getting

her back? She shrugged. Sometimes the words flooded out and sometimes they barely came in a trickle. I figured that was how it would be then.

"He's horrible. But I still love him too. He's my brother, right? He took care of me since I was little and there's always been a special thing between us." She looked away from me.

After a while, she said he made her sick too. Really deep-inside-her-body sick, like the plague. "If I stayed there anymore, I'd die. This is for real. It's the truth. I'd really and truly die if I stayed there anymore."

She poured sugar on her tongue and let it lie there, glistening, slowly dissolving in the afternoon light. She sprinkled on a little salt and the crystals mingled, bright white going to pure sun-gleam. Then something changed in her. Something like a wall broke and the words came pouring out.

FIFTY-SEVEN

"He uses me. That's what this is all about, Davi. He uses me, and if I'm not there to use then he might as well be dead. Like a light bulb uses electricity. Without it, what do you have? Some glass, some wires, and that twisty metal socket thing at the bottom. It's useless, right? It does nothing without the current. But when the electricity goes through it, you're not sitting there alone in the dark anymore. That's the way it is with me and my brother. Or like an instrument, a bassoon or clarinet maybe. Without the player's breath going into it, what do you have? Some wooden tubes and metal keys and contraptions that go up and down and it's totally useless. With the breath pouring through, it turns into beautiful music. You understand, Davi? He uses me and he has since before I can remember. I know it sounds like I'm in control if I'm the breath or the electricity. But that's not how it feels.

"He uses me. Like the master uses the slaves to pull on the oars and make the ship go skimming through the sea. You've seen those old galley ships, right? There's one in the Archbishop's museum from the ancient Empire days. With the battering ram in front for crashing into other warships and two eyes painted on the front, like the ship had a face and was alive. Fifty benches for the slaves to sit at, and they pulled those huge oars day and night to make the boat move. Just like your heart: never stopping, day and night, going all the time. Your body uses your heart, Davi. Without it, you're dead. And without me, my brother is dead. Or at least that's how it feels to him.

"He uses me. And he needs me to stay alive. That's what Lukas always said: every minute we were apart was like torture to him. He told me I was so important to him that every day I was away, when I ran off those other times, he could feel himself dying. So he must be already getting desperate. Not getting weaker, not for a while. But stronger, with that freak-out energy you get when you think you're going to die. Like somebody drowning in the sea, thrashing around and grabbing crazy, because they know it's going to end and if they don't get what they need, real fast, then it's over, really over. That must be how it feels."

FIFTY-EIGHT

I tried to make sense of this. At first it sounded like Lukas was a vampire, taking her blood to stay alive. Her words had such a dizzying effect on me that I even gave a quick glance at her neck, looking for marks. But she wasn't talking about glamorous fairy tales or brand-new big budget movies. And even though I was convinced that the two of us truly were mutations—*Homo lux*—I still knew the difference between film stars and real flesh and blood.

Was all this he-uses-me talk just a complicated way of saying how it felt? I asked her that. She just shrugged and poured another line of sugar onto her tongue. Her words came and her words went, like a faucet being turned off and on. Was all her talk about electricity and breath and slave-ships just a way of not really telling me what was true? It seemed like she'd been going round and round and not giving me the most important facts.

"What will do if he catches you, if he catches us together?"

"That can't happen. There's nothing more to it. It just can't."

"Look, you can stay here at the Angelus for a while

longer," I told her. "But with Carlos skulking around, and Herman's not going to stop him, soon enough he'll find you out." Carlos would sell her back to her brother if he didn't get enough money from me. Knowing how slimy he was, maybe he'd do both.

I was thinking of going straight to Lukas and trying to finish it. Maybe I could make a deal, I thought. Not with cash. I knew that was wrong, out of the question. But maybe I could trade or give him a substitute. Or if I really understood what he wanted, and why, maybe I could get Anna Z free some other way. I knew he might kill me. That part was for sure. But for the first time in my life, it hit me that there were worse things in the world than being dead. So getting up my nerve, I asked Anna Z to explain it to me one more time.

FIFTY-NINE

"You were right, before. It really was like being emptied out completely and filled up. With Django, at the show, I mean. When you saw me at the Maxima, I didn't know what my name was, where I'd been, or where I was going. They were doing 'She's the Hype,' I think, when it really hit me. My name and what I looked like, where I was and who I was. It all just vanished out of me. Did you ever see anybody playing with dry ice? It goes straight from solid to gas. That's called sublimation, going sublime. You take it out of the freezer and it vanishes into a white puff. *Whhffff!* And that's what it felt like when Rudy went into his solo and Django came out right to the edge of the stage and looked me in the eyes. I went sublime.

"Django was holding out his hand. Remember? Like he wanted everybody in the whole Maxima to touch him. Some of the girls were reaching for him. He had a purple scarf or a big fluttery ribbon. It went out over the crowd. Remember? The girls were stretching up for it. But not me, because I didn't need to. I was already with him, filled up as fast as I went sublime. Everything turned to vapor and whooshed away, and then everything rushed back inside me. Cosmic rays, the sound of Rudy's solo, Django's voice turned to light, the power and the gleam, and the alien specters passing through us all.

"I don't care anymore if something is possible or not. I just know what I saw and felt. The light went all silvery-gold. Electrum light, just like you saw this morning. And my body didn't weigh anything. There was nothing solid for gravity to grab onto and hold down. Solid, liquid, vapor and pure energy. The x-rays from a million miles away went streaming through me and through the whole world too.

"You know in 'The Man in the Moon in the Man' how Django says that something can be inside and outside at the same time? You look up at the moon and there's that face, right? Like right now. Look up there, Davi. Look. See? There's the face. But supposedly it's just craters and shadows, and the Apollonauts walked around there. But we make it into a face because we want everything to be human. You get that? Otherwise, it's like we can't even see it. So the Man in the Moon is really inside us. It's just something we make in our heads, and then we see it out there, up there, in the sky. I think maybe that's how it is with the Alien Drift. We want to see it in a way that makes some kind of sense. You said it looked like bombs falling, then angels, then spears. I don't think it's really any of that. And neither do you, right?

"It's like in 'Radiation Nation' on the second album. I never understood all the science and mythology in the verses. The chorus is what I love. It was what really got me and pulled me into the whole Django thing to start with.

The rising spirit quits the earth.
Up to the courts of light she flies.
Celestial legions guard her birth
and shout her welcome to the skies.

"The first time I heard that, it felt like Django was singing right to me and about me. The rising spirit was me. Django knew what was going on, even though I was just a girl in a city he'd never been to. Did that ever happen to you, Davi? You listen and it seems like every word and note and drumbeat—and even the silence—is about you and for you."

SIXTY

It wasn't until later that I realized she hadn't answered my question. Hearing all those words, I wanted to kiss her so bad. I wanted to hold onto her and feel her heart beating against mine, her body heat radiating through me. I suppose some people would say she was mentally disturbed, and a doctor might give her pills to calm down the crazy thoughts that were pouring out of her. But of course that would kill the thing in her that was so perfect.

And I thought about how Django said we see ourselves in other people's faces, like Anna Z was a mirror right then. Not that I wanted to kiss myself. That doesn't make any sense. But in a twisted kind of way I wanted to *be* Anna Z, even with Lukas hunting her down, and her fears and her crazy talk. I saw myself in her face, and it was okay. Better than okay. Way better.

Silent, standing there, she was perfect because I knew that there would always be more talk-talk-talking. Like a battery, all charged up, ready to connect with wires and send a sizzling zap into my brain again. All I had to do was touch her, make skin-to-skin contact, and she'd blast me with all that energy stored inside her. Alien, earth-girl, hidden, known to me and no one else: she was perfect.

I thought about what I'd seen at dawn the day before: electrum light and bright alien beings falling through the sky.

And even more than before, I wanted to kiss her. But she started talking again, and the words themselves felt like the light and sound combined into one force.

SIXTY-ONE

"The creature in the book is so lonely. He says he wants to have somebody else to share his life with, another creature like him. So he goes to the doctor, all freaked-out and frantic, and tells him to make a bride. When the doctor says no, the creature says he'll kill the doctor's new wife, he'll stalk him, and 'I shall be with you on your wedding night.' That's his curse. You understand? He'll show up on their wedding night. And in the movie, *The Bride of Frankenstein*, the same actress plays Mary Shelley and the bride. When I saw that the first time and figured out that they both were played by Elsa Lanchester, it was like a bomb going off in my brain. The writer, the girl Mary, is the bride of the creature. The one who dreamed up the whole story is the one who marries the creature. Or at least she's supposed to.

"I was the Bride of Frankenstein before I ever saw the movie or knew about Mary Shelley. It was me and my brother. Just us, together. Just us, alone in our house. You've seen him. You know what he looks like and how he acts. When he gets in one of his terrible moods, it's like the whole world is going to end. You know how good-looking he is. If he was a girl, you'd say he was beautiful, right? But when his feelings start pouring out, it's awful. Little kids start crying and dogs start whining. Business people close up their shops when he comes along. And it's not just the weird and intense that makes people want to get away. It's the scary and the crazy too. The wrong and the danger that glows around him. I'm not making this up, Davi. The Guardia go for the shock batons and call in to headquarters for backup. People go to church and pray just to wash the fear out of their nerves after they've seen him that way.

"You have any idea what that's like to live with, to *be* with all the time? I would've killed myself if I stayed there another week, and I swear on the Virgin that I'll kill myself if I have to go back to him. Mary Shelley never went back to her family. This is for real. Mary never went back and neither did the creature. They both got away clean and so can I. So can we, you and me. Right, Davi? Am I right? We're going to get away, and no one will ever find us and make us come back."

SIXTY-TWO

I told her I'd swear on the Virgin Mary too, if that's what she wanted. I'd swear that she never had to go back to her brother and live that way again. But swearing and talk-talk-talking and even kissing and holding onto her wouldn't do a thing to keep away Lukas, or make Carlos back down. We needed a plan. We needed real action.

So finally I showed her what I'd brought that day. It was the newspaper. Deep inside, with the TV listings, movie gossip from the New World, and music reviews was an article about Django Conn's tour. The headline read "The Great Conn Rules." It said that his was the most successful tour that summer—that he'd been selling out shows across the continent, and they'd added four more to meet the demand. Three of them were hundreds of miles away. But one was close enough that we could get there in a day. "I've already checked the train schedules," I told her. "I can get the money, and I've already done the calls for our tickets. Tomorrow we'll be gone. You and me, going to Django one more time."

If Anna Z thought I was great before, now I was the jewel on the crown and the ace of trumps. At first she kept shaking her head and saying she couldn't believe it. Then she jumped up and down and grabbed me and swung me around and said I was the best thing that had ever happened to her. We were going to Django, to see and hear and be there for the last day of the tour. And nothing could make her happier or give her more hope.

"Are we coming back afterward?" she asked.

I couldn't really answer that. I'd lived my whole life in the city, and it was hard, really hard, to picture myself starting a life in a new place. I'd never gotten past the city limits. I'd never even taken a boat ride far enough out that the city was lost over the horizon. Of course, my father had gone off on business trips, and Sabina had traveled some too, with Carlos and Cyanne and their friends. Skiing in the mountains, wintering in cooler locales, gambling at the Azure Coast casinos. I'd had that choice too, but I'd stayed put at the Angelus. I couldn't imagine never coming back. But I also couldn't imagine leaving Anna Z there and never seeing her again.

SIXTY-THREE

The train left the St. Paulus station at ten the next morning. The show was at eight that night. We had plenty of time. The only real problem was getting out of the Angelus and to the station without anyone seeing us. Carlos would surely be skulking around the hotel. And her brother—I had no idea where he'd be or what he was up to.

I told Anna Z to stay in the suite with the doors locked and not to make any noise. There were arrangements I had to take care of, and it would be a lot easier if I made them alone. Money, mostly, was what we needed. New clothes we could buy. Food and a place to stay were no problem if we had the funds.

It was late afternoon by the time we said goodbye. Sadness hit me hard as I heard her slide the dead bolt on the door. Walking along the dim hallway was sadder, all by myself again. Sneaking down the stairs and back to the main lobby felt like drifting through oblivion. Not like waking from a dream, but moving from one dream to another. Anna Z was more real than anyone I'd ever known. When I was with her that was for sure. Now, going about the hotel, I felt a twinge of doubt, a flicker of unbelief.

Still, I stayed with our plan. Money was the most important thing. So I went to the main desk and asked Armand if he could give me a cash voucher. He never asked why I needed money, but he did make it hard, with his pinched lips and twitching fingers. He stared over the tops of his eyeglasses as if I were some hideous specimen in a museum. When I told him how much I wanted, his eyebrows arched up into thin, black curves. He didn't argue. He also didn't write the voucher, at least not yet.

I made up some lies about buying skis and going with Sabina to the mountains. "We've been planning this for weeks. It's for my birthday." I even mentioned how my father forgot it sometimes, trying to play on Armand's well-hidden soft spot. I named some resorts and hotels. We haggled back and forth a little. "And you know how much my father hates dealing with petty cash," I reminded him. Armand made a counteroffer, mostly I think to save his pride, and I accepted the voucher without another word.

SIXTY-FOUR

After a stop at the cashier's office, I headed to the east kitchen. Fabian was surprised when I asked him for a loan. He knew I was good for it, of course, and trusted that he'd get his money back in full. Maria-Claire came in, pushing her room service cart full of empty dishes, and I hit her up for some cash too. She gave me one of her sad, inquiring looks. "You're not in trouble, are you Davi?"

"No, I just want to buy a new turntable. A Stennheizer 411. That's a really good one."

She knew this was a lie but didn't press me on it. She gave me all the money she had on her. Then a call came in from above, and she went to prepare her serving table for the delivery. Plates, silverware, napkins, a vase with fresh-cut lavender and anemones, a finger bowl, and a selection of sliced lemons and oranges. She nodded to say goodbye and rolled her cart down toward the ovens.

My last stop before packing was Sabina's rooms. It seemed to me that either way—if Carlos was there or not—I'd be able to get some money from my sister. He might even help persuade her, figuring that I was collecting money to pay him off and keep him quiet.

I knocked and got no response. "It's me." I was using my let-me-in voice. "Open up, okay? We need to talk." More silence. I pressed my ear against the door and knocked again. "I know you're in there." This wasn't true. I didn't hear a thing inside, but it felt good to say it, to sound strong, in charge, unafraid.

When I got to my room, there was Carlos, sitting with a wine bottle at his feet and the phone in his lap. He stared at me with the cold, soulless eyes of a hungry snake. "I had a little talk with Lukas today. He's unhappy, very unhappy. You understand? He really wants the girl back. He said I should call him as soon I saw you. So talk. Now."

"I don't know what you mean." My big voice was gone.

"Don't play stupido with me, Davi. This is getting very serious." He pulled back one sleeve and showed me his arm. "Take a look. He's a crazy man. This is what he did to me for just asking a couple questions about his sister." A half dozen red welts shone on the inside of his arm. "Cigar burns. He held my arm down and got me six times before I could pull away. Just because I said I could see why you liked Anna Z. He'll kill you, Davi. That's for sure. I hardly looked at her, and he was ready to burn my eyes out. That makes it a lot worse for you, right? He was going to blind me just for saying how good Anna Z looked. I didn't even touch her. I just said she had something special, and he started grinding me with the cigar."

He put his finger on the phone dial. "Where is she?"

I looked away, toward the window, as though something out there might save me.

"You're not going anywhere until I've given Lukas what

he wants. I'm not getting blinded over this. I thought I could make a little cash, but I'm not dying over a messed-up girl. So just tell me—where is she?"

The room was bathed with late afternoon light. Silver, gold, copper, lead, mercury, bronze: all the ancient metals shone in the sky. A record album lay on my turntable, catching the weird rays, gleaming with pure alien light. I knew which disc it was: *Gimme Back My Phantom Limbs*. I turned on the amp and set the needle down in the groove. For a few seconds, the air in the room seemed to vibrate the way a gong or bell vibrates. Then Django's voice came wailing from the speakers.

SIXTY-FIVE

This, Carlos hadn't expected. Maybe an argument, maybe whiny excuses or lies or threats of calling in Hermann and the detectives. Or I might've just run away. None of those occurred to me in the moment. All that I cared about right then was music, the voice captured on vinyl and the voice I'd soon be hearing from huge stage speakers.

I suppose it's simple. I went toward the thing I knew and loved. I had no real weapons to fight back with. Yes, I knew the ins and outs of the Angelus better than anyone. And hiding Anna Z was important. But as soon as we left the hotel, that would be useless. On the train, in a new city where I'd never been, at the show, what I'd depended on my whole life would be gone. So it was music, glam loudness, wild voices, and freaky baryton riffs that I went toward.

Carlos got up, kicking the wine bottle across the room. He threw the phone to the floor and yelled at me to turn down the music. My hand went to the volume knob and doubled the sound. Furious now, he came at me, shouting and waving a fist. I shouted back at him, "I can't hear you!" And that was true. He reached for the turntable, and I pushed him away. Cursing, he tried again to yank the needle out of the groove.

Django was crying above the gamba: "I sing aloud the silent hymns. Gimme Back My Phantom Limbs." And as the baryton delved down and blasted on its lowest string, Carlos got past me, grabbed the tone arm and pulled it off the record. The needle sliced across the grooves, with a screeching explosion of noise. Django and the band disappeared. The disc kept spinning, dead silent now. Carlos had broken the tone arm right off the stereo. He tossed this to the floor and growled, "Tell me where the girl is."

Getting no response, he reached down to the turntable. His greasy fingers fumbled at the record. This I couldn't stand. I had a second or two, as he turned his back to me. The sky's metallic light flooded into me. Something passed through me: Anna Z's energy, glam specters, alien spirit, or the echo of Django's voice? I had no name for it then. No words and no clear pictures in my head. I grabbed the first thing that came to hand, Carlos's wine bottle, and slammed it hard on the back his head. He tottered, turning to look at me. I hit him again, this time on the side of his head, and he crumpled to the floor.

Then I heard Sabina snarling at me, crazy with fear and hate. She'd been standing in the doorway, I saw, as Carlos and I fought. How long had it taken? Maybe a few seconds. Too little time for her to join in and help him. She wore a loose, silk dressing gown. Her hair was a mess, and her feet were bare. Her snarling fell to a faint hiss, making my name into something obscene. She pushed at me, getting me away from Carlos, then knelt down and listened for his breath. I was out of there and halfway down the hall before the thought hit me that I might've killed him. Turning back would've been useless though. I'd done what I'd done, and nothing could ever change that.

SIXTY-SIX

It wasn't panic that flooded through me, or guilt, or even fear. What I felt was powerful, overwhelming, but there was no pain in it. Nothing wrong. Everything good. The light still shone, though bolting down the stairs, I couldn't see it. The sound was still there, hidden in the grooves of the record, even if I couldn't hear it. What Anna Z had talked about so much was freedom. Now, for the first time, I understood what she meant. The life I'd had was ending. Right then and there, as I snuck down a service hallway, the world was shifting and changing forever. I was about to lose my life as I knew it. We'd leave the city the next morning, and I could never come back. This was freedom.

I made it to the suite and did our code-knock so Anna Z would know it was me. I slipped inside, locked the door behind me, and whispered her name. There was no answer. I said her name out loud, and now the panic began to bubble up. She wasn't there. I searched the whole suite. Bedroom, bathroom, kitchen, the balcony. *Now* I let myself feel the loss completely.

Anna Z had vanished. Maybe Lukas had come and taken her. Or worse, maybe she'd gone to him and told him our whole plan. I'd get caught and go to prison for killing Carlos. My father would abandon me, and that would be the end.

Where now was the shimmering presence I'd seen in the sky and felt pass through me? Nowhere.

I was a fool. I'd always been a fool. I was nothing and nobody. I'd gotten stone-drunk on Anna Z's voice, done the stupidest things I could possibly do, and now I was all alone. Sabina would laugh as they took me away. My father would just stand there with that cold, empty look on his face.

I took the roll of cash out of my pocket, and undoing the rubber band, tossed the money into the air. The bank notes floated around me like confetti. Reds and blues, greens and oranges, yellows and purples. I collapsed onto the floor and lay there like someone who'd won the Archbishop's lottery and died of a heart attack surrounded by his winnings.

Then I heard the glass doors to the balcony open and there was Anna Z. She looked bad: worn-out, freaked-out, and afraid. The shine from the sky made her glasses into two circles of hard glare. Or maybe what came in through my eyes and went into my brain was scrambled by interference. What I was feeling—furious and overjoyed at the same time—surely messed with what I saw. I ran over and put my arms around her, shaking and saying her name. Again and again. Relief, confusion, happiness boiled through my body like jets of steam through a pressure valve.

SIXTY-SEVEN

"I'm sorry, Davi. I know I shouldn't have done it. I'm really sorry but I called Lukas."

"Why?" I moaned. "Why would you do that?"

"I had to do it. We're going tomorrow, and I thought I might never see him again. So I called."

"But he wants to kill me!"

"I don't know if I should've or shouldn't. But I did it. I knew he'd be getting desperate, so I thought it would be best for everybody if I told him I was all right. Best for him, but for you and me too. I thought if he wasn't all crazy with worry, he wouldn't try to find us. Wait, wait, just let me finish. I didn't tell him where I was or where we're going. Don't worry. He'll never find us. I promise. But I had to say goodbye.

"Then as soon as I hung up, the second the phone was off, I heard footsteps in the hallway, and I thought it was him. I know that's ridiculous, but it's the way my mind works sometimes. When I was little, I was positive that Lukas could be two places at once. He told me he could do it and I believed him. He said he could read my thoughts, and he even went into my dreams sometimes. Or at least he claimed he did. He said he could look around in my mind when I was sleeping. And see absolutely everything. So you've got to understand this, Davi. I was never alone, even when there was nobody else in the room and my door was locked. I spent my whole life with my brother doing that to me: messing with my mind and watching me even when it wasn't possible. I don't think anymore it was real. It couldn't be. But when I was little, I just accepted it.

"So thinking about going away forever . . . I lost it. I just went . . . I didn't know what I was doing. And then talking to Lukas kicked the old feelings in, and when I heard the footsteps, I freaked-out and went up to the roof. I thought it was him, and I had to get away."

She'd tangled one finger in her hair, turning it, yanking as she talked. "He tried everything on me. Three minutes on the phone and it was like I was back there with him locked in my room. He said that he needed me and so it was wrong for me to go away. Every minute I was gone was killing him. After all we'd had together, how could I do this to him? And for anybody who helped me, it would end up really bad. Did I want you to get hurt, really bad hurt? He kept saying your name, Davi, saying it slow and quiet like he was trying to decide what to do to you when he caught us. And when I didn't answer, he said he knew what I was thinking. That's when I hung up. It was like I was a little kid again, and he was reading my mind. I could almost feel him in there, looking around in my thoughts. It must've been you coming down the hall that I heard and I lost it. I had to run. I'm sorry, Davi. I'm really sorry."

SIXTY-EIGHT

Holding her close, I told her it was okay. All I cared about was that she hadn't gone away. Calling her brother didn't matter much now because we had to get out of there as soon as we could. I explained what had happened in my room. And I said that I didn't even know if Carlos was still alive. "Probably the Guardia are already here at the hotel. Hermann will keep them from making a big scene. There won't be any sirens or squads of uniformed men rushing around. But for sure they've been called in by now."

At last, I let her go and said we had to get moving. With a heavy sigh, she agreed. We gathered up the cash and made two rolls now, one for each of us. After wrapping up a little food and brushing away our footprints from the dusty carpets, we were gone. I took the TV and fan mags with me to dump in the first storeroom that was open. If Hermann or the Guardia thought to look in the suite, they'd know it had been used recently. But if they weren't positive it had been us, it might help.

I'd lost my invisibility. By then the word had surely gone out to the staff that the detectives were looking for me. Our plan now was to find the maid's uniform Anna Z had worn before and a big laundry cart. She would change back into the frumpy dress and cap. I'd get into the cart and she'd cover me with towels and sheets and push me into one of the service elevators. In the lowest basement, I thought, we could take a detour away from the laundry rooms and leave the Angelus through one of the delivery tunnels. We'd go to the train station and spend the night there in some secluded corner of a waiting room.

None of our plans had worked out exactly. I suppose they never do. This one shifted quickly, twisted, and then broke. When I'd asked Maria-Claire for a loan, I must've said something about leaving the city. Or she'd figured it out from the way I was acting. In any case, there she was in the stairway, looking for us.

"Were you really the one, Davi?" She reached out and brushed the hair away from my eyes. "Did you do it?" She seemed more sad than surprised. "You gave it to Carlos on the head?"

"Is he dead?"

"No, I don't think so. They took him off to the hospital. Hermann is keeping the whole thing hush-hush. It's going to be a lot safer," Maria-Claire said, "for you to stay here than to wander the streets all night. I'll come and get you when the way is clear."

Maria-Claire had always taken good care of me and I trusted her. The kitchen was mostly where we saw each other. But over the years she'd hidden me when my tutor was hunting me out for more tedious lessons. She'd sworn to my father, once, that I wasn't the one who'd tracked canal mud on a newly cleaned red carpet. And she'd even taken the blame for an oriental vase that got broken in one of my fights with Sabina. This was obviously a hundred times more serious, but I got the same feeling from her as before. I, *we*, could count on her.

"Be careful, Davi. You hear me? Take care of yourself." She smiled at Anna Z. "And her too. Keep her safe."

I told Anna Z that we'd be all right one more night there and headed back to the secret suite.

SIXTY-NINE

"In *Frankenstein*, there's another reason why the creature said to the doctor, 'I shall be with you on your wedding night.' It wasn't just because he was furious and crazy with loneliness and wanted his revenge. Like I said before, he wanted a bride for himself, and the doctor told him 'no.' He wouldn't make another creature. But there was something else going on. Doctor Frankenstein was going to marry Elizabeth Lavenza. And you know who she was, Davi? His sister. That's in the book. Right there in black and white. She wasn't his real biological sister with the same genes. She was an orphan. His parents took her in, and they lived together as kids in the same house. They grew up together, and they were going to get married and spend the rest of their lives that way. He calls her 'My more than sister— the beautiful and adored companion—mine—mine—to protect, love and cherish.' This is right out of the book. I'm not making any of this up. I read it so many times I have it all by heart.

"I thought it was so romantic when I was a kid. *Beautiful and adored. To protect and love and cherish.* What girl wouldn't want that? Living with my brother, that kind of thing was exactly what I wanted to hear. You understand me, Davi? 'My more than sister.' I picked the book up the first time because of the creature. I was little and thought he was great in the movies. Growling and stomping around and killing. But the book is really different. It's all about deep feelings. Page after page of it. That's what kept me going back. *Beautiful and adored. To protect and love and cherish.* That's what it was like for Lukas and me. At least some of the time.

"So when the creature says he'll come to the doctor's house on the night of his wedding, it's not just about revenge. He's the hand of Fate, and you know what Fate does to guys who want to marry their sisters? Even if there's none of the same genes or chromosomes or any kind of real family connection, once you use the words 'sister' and 'marry' together, you're calling in Fate's avenger. And what he does is real simple, Davi. He kills the girl and leaves the doctor crazy with grief for the rest of his life."

SEVENTY

We'd spent a couple of hours sitting in the main room of the suite, not saying much. After Maria-Claire had left, I'd brought the TV back and we flipped through the channels for a while. Of course nothing on TV could push away our thoughts and feelings. Game shows, political news, sports, idiot comedies about idiotic families. None of these seemed real. I shut it off, and we made some small talk about Django and the concert, how great it was going to be and how free we'd feel. But that petered out to nothing. As the sun was going down, we stood at the glass doors to the balcony. There it was, the glow of electrum light. There they came, the spectral words pouring out of Anna Z.

It didn't make me afraid to hear her talk about Frankenstein and her brother, or sad or angry or even confused now. It seemed like I understood. Her brother had gotten inside her. Into her mind, her thoughts, her dreams, into the secret place where dreams come from. Down, down deep. *Beautiful and adored. To protect and love and cherish.*

Since they were little kids, they'd been together in their own secret world. Just the two of them. Anna Z and Lukas and no one else. For years, right or wrong, they'd been together in their own private, hidden place. I almost envied her. No, not *almost*—I really did wish I'd had her life. No one had ever cared that much about me, even if that caring was all wrong. He'd been together with her in a way I'd never really understand. But one day it was just too much. She knew it had to end. And so she called up Frankenstein—the creature—to be her knight in shining armor, to come and save the day. I know that's twisted around. How could killing Elizabeth the sister-bride save her? How could a creature made out of dead body parts be the big hero? What did a book written centuries ago have to do with Anna Z, with her and me?

Standing at the windows as the metallic light claimed the skies, I got a glimpse of who and what Anna Z really was. She'd told me the whole truth about herself. I'd told her the truth too. I'd never lied to her, not once. That was the reason, more even than loving Django, that the two of us had to stay together. We never lied. She made up stories. Her ideas went skidding and skating all over the place. But that's different, totally different, than telling me a lie. Frankenstein was just a book, all of it made up. But it wasn't a lie. There was something true in the book, something deep and real, just like her talk-talk-talking was true.

SEVENTY-ONE

Darkness came. The city changed before us as we stood there. Buildings blurred, then disappeared. Lights, hundreds and thousands, emerged like the constellations looming out of the night sky. Anna Z said, "I found a way up to the roof from the balcony. You want to go up there? It's pretty amazing."

"Together?"

"Of course. You and me."

"Sure."

She grabbed a blanket and a pillow off the bed. I opened the balcony door and the sounds of the city were suddenly much more distinct. Church bells, double iron wheels on the cobblestone street, a man singing with a voice like a wooden flute, night birds, a train whistle. We slid over the low stone balcony wall, inched along a ledge, and went up an iron fire escape ladder. She stopped suddenly, and I thought for a second that we'd been found out. But she pulled me close and kissed me on the cheek. Her laugh, then, was like a special gift, something she'd offer only to me. She'd fled from Lukas and their secret world. And now it was just her and me.

Tugging on my hand, she led me across the lumpy, tarred surface of a roof. There was one more above that. Another iron ladder, this one wobbling as we climbed. Half the bolts that fastened it to the wall had rusted free. She went first, with the blanket wrapped around her like a billowing cloak. I had the pillow, tucked under one arm. She went over the edge. I followed and there was our private rooftop.

The Angelus was more than a hundred years old. Over that time, towers, wings, buttresses, skylights, a chapel, and a penthouse had been added. So around and below us the hotel looked more like a small city than a single, huge building. Beyond that, the city proper extended as far as we could see. Still, this rooftop was a hidden place where no one could see us.

The moon was up, the sun's secret mirror. Anna Z said something about the solar rays going out gold, hitting the moon, and coming back to us converted into lunar silver. I was listening as best I could. But as she spoke about celestial light, she was taking off her clothes. She told me about getting a moon-tan, how good it felt to be open and free in the glow of the night sky. I tried to listen and understand. But what I saw standing there before me was making my head spin and my heart slam. I don't mean there was anything wrong about it. Or that I hadn't looked at pictures in the galleries and at the white marble statues of beautiful girls wearing almost nothing. I couldn't go ten feet into a museum without seeing nude goddesses, naked mermaids, nymphs clothed in nothing but moonbeams. But Anna Z was real, alive, warm, and only for me.

SEVENTY-TWO

Totally open to the sky and to my eyes, she took my hand and said, "I'm a virgin. There it is, Davi. I said it. I really am still a virgin." Her voice was like the private roar of a seashell pressed to my ear.

"There's power in that, real power. You know the statues in the churches, Mary with the blue dress and the halo and that look on her face like she's totally lost it? Emptied out and filled back up again. I hardly ever go to church, but whenever I've been there, what really gets me are those statues of the Virgin Mary. I know exactly what she was feeling now when she became the Mother of God. Still a virgin but totally changed. I think that's what you saw in my face at the Maxima. It happened when Django looked out at the crowd, and his eyes met mine. I mean that for real. He looked right at me when Rudy was doing his solo on 'She's the Hype,' and he knew all about me. What I was and what I wasn't. What I had been and what I could be. What I *was*, now that the change had happened.

"I didn't lie to you before, and I'm not going to now. I'm a virgin. Running off those other times was real. I wasn't making that up. I really did and it totally freaked Lukas out because he thought that when he found me I wouldn't be a virgin anymore. And if I'm not a virgin, then I'm nothing. That's what he thinks. And if I'm nothing, then so is he. But that wasn't why I ran. I kept thinking about Mary Shelley and how she ran off and what came of that: Frankenstein. If she could do it then so could I. That's why I went the first two times. Because of Frankenstein and making the creature. But the third time was about Django and *being* a creature.

"I loved the story since I was a little kid. I got a hold of everything Frankenstein: comic books, records, coloring books, posters, stickers, movies. I had green makeup, fake scars, and neck bolts for Christmas and All Saints. There's something amazing about the creature. He's horrible and beautiful at the same time. You know what I mean? You can't look at him, and you can't look away.

"Then I found out about Mary Shelley and how brave and wild and free she made herself. Think about that. A seventeen-year-old virgin and she ran away from home forever. She was just a teenager when she created the man who made the creature. There's a line in the book that hit me, and I've never forgotten it. Mary says 'a sudden light broke in upon me—a light so brilliant and wondrous, yet so simple.' Light! You understand what I'm talking about, Davi? She saw the light too. She saw the specters and maybe even the Alien Drift. Sometimes I think it comes and goes, like a tide. You know what I mean? In and out.

"And later on in the book she says, 'It had then filled me with a sublime ecstasy that gave wings to the soul and allowed it to soar from the obscure world to light and joy.'

That's us. That's you and me." She took my hand, tugging me closer. "Souls with wings. Soaring. Light and joy. That's what I ran away to find, and you were there, at the show, when I found it.

"Mary Shelley was a virgin when she wrote the book. Later on, she had kids and got married, and she never wrote anything good after that. Only one book that mattered and she wrote it when she was like me. Don't you see? She had to be a virgin to make the creature. Not because of keeping her body pure, or right and wrong, like the priests say in church. This isn't about rules and your body being the temple of the Holy Spirit. It's not about being untouched. The creature was born in her mind, or in her heart maybe. From thought and feeling, not from her body like ordinary people. Look, I know this is a lot, probably too much, for you to get. But you're the first person I ever met who was willing to listen and understand. Or at least try to understand."

SEVENTY-THREE

I looked at her body and then inside my own thoughts. I tried to tell her what I was feeling. Fear, longing, hope and hopelessness, and maybe something like love. But it came out all garbled, my words just as stammering as my thoughts. She shrugged, I think, and told me that I should do it too. Take off my clothes and feel the moon's rays on my skin.

"Me too," I told her after a while. "I'm a virgin too." Saying it felt good, not bragging or making apologies but just saying what was true. She nodded and said she knew that already and that she didn't mind. It was something good about me, something that set me apart from all the others.

The only thing she left on were her glasses, two moon-pale circles, framed by the wildness of her black hair. She was no goddess. I know that. She was just a girl who was willing to let everything go. *That* was what I found so powerful, so wonderful about her. Her body wasn't perfect, I suppose. But I didn't care at all about gorgeous goddesses or movie stars. All that mattered was right there in front of me. She'd let go and was truly herself, not questioning or fighting it. And she wanted me to be the same.

I should've been embarrassed. I wasn't. I should've turned away or looked out at the city instead of at Anna Z. I didn't.

She stood there, white as polished marble. I looked and I looked some more, and when she told me again to take off my clothes, that's what I did. Then she took the pillow from me, spread the blanket on the rough tarred roof, and said I should lie down with her. This was our time and our place, and nobody in the whole world could take it away from us. The air was warm and the moon's rays cool, like a breeze, on my bare skin. So I did it. I joined her there on the blanket. We lay together, barely touching. Just a few strands of her hair on my shoulder, fingertip to fingertip, and her hip hardly grazing mine. And as I relaxed, I felt the heat, or the energy of her body radiating into me.

We lay there a long time, saying nothing. The moon watched us, or at least that was how it felt. Was there a Man in the Moon in the Man staring down? I'd never really understood that song. With Anna Z, though, lying close together, it seemed like I got a better glimpse of what Django had meant.

> *What's in is out.*
> *What's far is near.*
> *What feels so real*
> *and crystal clear*
> *are pictures which*
> *all live within.*
> *And if you doubt,*
> *they disappear.*

Anna Z was real. I never once doubted that. Still, it also felt like she was something I'd called up from somewhere deep inside myself. Even more bizarre, I thought: could both be true? Real and warm, a naked girl's body just as I'd imagined it. And also a beautiful white-gold specter that might've been just a dream of bright lunacy. She told me about the word later, how in the old days, the Frankenstein time, everyone thought that the moon made people crazy.

Luna, the moon. Lunar and lunacy.

I thought about moving closer, of course. How could I not think that? I pictured running my hand over her body, just as they did in the films, pulling her nearer. If I was honest with myself, I'd have to admit I'd been thinking about this since the moment I'd seen her at the Maxima. That night on the rooftop, that feeling I had lying beside her was perfect. It was also fragile. I knew that one little wrong move would wreck it all. Staying in our balance of close and far, together and separate, was what really made that time so powerful. So I lay there with Anna Z until a calmness filled me and sleep took us both.

SEVENTY-FOUR

When I awoke, the stars were still out, but the moon had disappeared. A quake of panic surged through me. The blanket was folded over me, and Anna Z was no longer there. I sat up, dizzy and confused. I called for her. I got up, yanking the blanket around me like a toga. Quietly, she said my name and told me everything was okay. I peered into the early morning darkness. There she was, dressed again, sitting by a low stone wall. I found my clothes, and now I was embarrassed, going to the far side of the rooftop to put them on.

From there, I could see in all four directions. It took me a moment, turning slowly, to find the east. No dawn light was rising yet, but it wouldn't be long. Had Maria-Claire already come to the suite below to say it was time to leave? Were the Guardia swarming the Angelus? Or worse—had her brother gotten into the hotel and found a trail to our hiding place? I had no idea and neither did Anna Z. We had no choice but to go back the way we'd come: down the ladder, which seemed more wobbly now, across the lower rooftop, along the ledge, and back through the balcony.

The door was still locked, and there was no note from

Maria-Claire. I said we should get going, right then. The bakers and some of the maids would be coming on duty soon. Other than them, the only people we'd likely pass were those staggering home from parties, and they'd be in no shape to recognize me, let alone give us any trouble.

However, we weren't quite ready yet. It seemed that we both had something to say. Neither one of us could do it, though.

I unlocked the door but didn't open it. Anna Z asked if I had my roll of cash. I showed her mine, and she showed me hers. I said again we should leave and she agreed. Maybe it was just simple fear that held us back. We both knew her brother might be waiting anywhere along the route to the train station. This could be our last moment, just the two of us together. And maybe we hung back because we were afraid of losing it. I wanted to tell her how perfect it had been, up on the roof with her, open to the sky and safe, open to each other and doubly safe. Even that, I couldn't get out now. Fear and doubt ate at my thoughts. Adrenaline buzzed in my veins, my stomach, my brain. I said a third time we should leave and turned the doorknob.

SEVENTY-FIVE

The corridor was empty. We rode a slow, shaking elevator and went down a hallway with lights that hummed louder as we passed beneath each fixture. A maid who I'd never seen before bowed her head as we went by, as though we were the royalty of the manor. An old man in evening clothes sat in a huge overstuffed chair, singing a nursery rhyme quietly to himself. He put his hand to his head, as if tipping an invisible hat. We took a back passageway around the lobby, down to the east kitchen.

There was Maria-Claire, setting up her cart with someone's early morning breakfast, fiddling with the flowers. She saw me and came over to give me a hug. "I was just on my way up to get you," she whispered and took us into a big pantry. "As far as I can tell, the way out is clear. I haven't seen any sign of the Guardia. I heard that Carlos is going to be all right. Hermann hasn't brought any extra detectives on duty." I described Lukas to her, and she shook her head. "No. I haven't seen him."

She'd gone into her savings and gotten more money for me. At first, I refused to accept any more. But she insisted. "Take it, Davi. You're going to need all you can get." Handing the folded wad of bank notes over, sadness seemed to well up inside her. "Where exactly are you going?" she wanted to know. I didn't say. "When will you be back?" I had no answer for that either. So she kissed me on the forehead, a motherly goodbye kiss, and said I should write when things had settled down.

Following the path out that she'd already checked, we left the Angelus, going from the closed-in darkness of a tunnel to the huge open darkness of the sky. A canal flowed inky black before us, carrying the starlight out to the sea. We were free, gone, escaped. The train station was only ten blocks away.

But it took a lot longer to get there than on any other normal day. Lukas knew where I lived, and he'd claimed he'd seen Anna Z leaving the Angelus that first night. If he was as wild to get her back as she said, he could be lurking somewhere nearby.

So every block we traveled was like crossing the dead zone between two armies. Maybe no threat waited for us, or maybe Lukas would come raging out of the shadows, exploding like a bomb. We went down some alleys tangled with sagging laundry lines. We cut through somebody's workshop, strewn with scrap metal and broken tools. We had to tiptoe by an old lady who slept on the pavement. One of her eyes, swollen and gummy, opened as we passed. "Never, never, never," she muttered, and laughed like a hissing cobra.

"This way," Anna Z said, taking my hand. "The station's over there." She was right. The building was huge and gray, smudged to a blur by the smoke of ten thousand trains. We found a side entrance and headed for the lobby.

Neither one of us had ever traveled far by train before. I'd seen movies, though; I'd read books, and I knew about schedules and tickets. It took a little while to figure out the huge board in the main lobby. Between us, we did it and soon were sitting on a cold wooden bench in the farthest, darkest corner of a side waiting room. Three hours had to pass before we could board the train. Then came a hundred miles of track, speed and rocking rhythm, every second taking us closer to Django. Anna Z put her arm around me, leaned her head close to mine, and whispered in my ear that she'd never been happier in her whole life.

SEVENTY-SIX

"When I was little, I used to imagine running away, far away, and it looked exactly like this. A train station with people coming and going. Like the couple over there. See them? Saying goodbye, so romantic, so sad, their last kiss. Or the girl that just came in. The one with the long, dowdy coat. Did you even notice her? I'd imagine that I could sneak away—like her—and no one would pay any attention to me. That's a big part of it, just being left alone. And when we get there, Davi, absolutely nobody will know us. That's what I wanted when I was little. To be left alone. And when I got older, I wanted it even more.

"The first time I left, I only went a couple of blocks away from home. I kept asking myself why not go, go, go? Put a thousand miles behind me. Farther—as far as I could. Why not put as much distance between me and my brother as I could? Maybe go all the way to the New World. But of course, I didn't. And I ended up back home with Lukas breathing down my neck worse than ever. More rules, more control and suspicion. The second time was better, more hidden. Still, I was right here in the city. And people knew me. Lukas had seen me talking to Jules before I left. There was no way it would work out.

"I get it now, Davi, why I didn't go to the end of the continent those other times. Or around the globe. I understand now. You're it. You're the reason. I think I knew deep inside that I needed somebody else to run away with. Somebody exactly right. And you're it. You're the reason I stayed and the reason I'm going away.

"There was a game we played when I was little. It wasn't a game that anybody lost or won, like chess or the Tombola, but there were rules and a way of playing it right or wrong. We called it 'doing an experiment.' Lukas was always in charge, saying what I should do and when. Like a lot of kids, we started out playing doctor. With our parents gone, it was easy. But then it got different, more and more like the book and the movie. Lukas was Doctor Frankenstein, and I was the creature. *His* creature. In a way, it was like he was inventing me, making me up out of his mind. Out of his thoughts and his feelings too.

"I liked doing the experiments, at least at first. He had a special room he called his lab on the top floor of our house. He had it all set up just for the experiments. I'd lie on the table, and Lukas would cover me up with a big white cloth. I had to be quiet, perfectly silent, lying there under the cloth. Like I was dead. Then he'd shine a bright light. He'd pull back the cloth and tell me how beautiful I was. And that was the best thing I ever had, Davi. Feeling like there was nothing and nobody in the whole world as beautiful and perfect as me.

"It was the best and the worst. Because more and more

it made me feel awful too, especially when Lukas got inside me and knew all my thoughts and how I felt. Just Lukas and me, alone together. We got older and the game changed. It got stranger. I remember the big, bright light and how it felt like the rays were going right through me. And it started to go on longer too, Lukas and me and all that silence in the lab like a tomb. That was a big part of the game. I could never say a word the whole time we were playing, never make a sound.

"But what we're doing, Davi, is the opposite, and that's why I know it's right and good for me to run away this time and this way. No more silence. I can say whatever I want now. I can tell the truth, the whole truth, at least to you. When we get there, all the old games will be over. When we get there, we can do anything. We can change our names. We can be whoever we want. One night with Django and the wild mutation, and then who knows what we'll turn into? Last night the moon was just about full. That means tonight is the night—total lunar spectral glow. It's going to be amazing, Davi. *We're* going to be amazing. I can feel it already. The light from last night is still in me, and it's in you too. We'll be at the show and we'll *be* the show."

SEVENTY-SEVEN

She kept going on like that for a long time. And even though I loved to hear it, all those words—repeated and twisted around on themselves, rising from a whisper to a kind of woozy singsong—started to scare me a little. She wasn't going crazy or telling herself lies so strong that she started to believe them. She wasn't losing her mind as she kept on talk-talk-talking. It was more like she was *making her mind*, right there with me, making herself out of words. Beginning, middle, and end: like a movie. The theme music, the opening shot of the film, the credits, and now the big escape scene. She was creating herself, like a movie creating pictures and voices in the darkness of the theater. From nothing to the biggest, wildest *something* I'd ever known.

Suddenly, she was quiet. She pulled me close and put her lips to mine. We kissed, hard and long. Her breath went into me and mine went into her. The whole world fell away like the dissolve shot, where the camera focuses on one thing and rest of the scene goes blurry and disappears. No words anymore. No sounds at all. It was just me and Anna Z. Then she pulled away a little bit, and we sat there, forehead to forehead, as though her thoughts could go straight from her brain into mine. I let it happen, or maybe I just pretended. Either way, it felt the same. I could see what was inside her mind. I could hear the words without her saying them out loud.

If before she made me feel dizzy and weird—now I was totally drunk. Over the years, I'd seen hundreds of people at the Angelus who'd had too much wine and spirits. They staggered and giggled, talked too loud or whispered like lunatics. They danced real close and slow in the great ballroom. Very romantic. Once, a man in his evening clothes opened the window, climbed out on the ledge, and stood there all night yelling at the sky about some girl he loved and lost. Hermann's men got him back in eventually. I'd seen the whole thing from my window, and it was sad when his yelling stopped. His voice had been so free, so overflowing with what he felt. That's how I was with Anna Z at the station. Drunk, though I'd never even tasted wine.

SEVENTY-EIGHT

The train came and we got on. It went and we went with it. We sat together, holding hands, as the train gathered speed in the tunnel and then broke out into daylight. The city flashed by. I saw a few buildings I knew, though from the backs they seemed very different. We crossed the Great Canal. Then we were beyond, out in the countryside.

We saw very little of it, though, sitting together like two refugees on the last train out of Doomsville. Knee to knee and shoulder to shoulder, we huddled in the last seat of the last car. We made three stops, and still a hundred miles didn't take very long. The train started the journey in a dark tunnel and ended in one too. With a blast of steam and squealing brakes, a long lurch and a sudden jolt, we were there.

The crowds in the station flowed upward, and we flowed with them. Stairs and passageways, long corridors with low ceilings, then emerging into a great lobby where the chandelier hung like a glittering spaceship coming down for a landing. Only then did I really feel the truth. We'd made it. We were there. And in only a few hours, we'd be at the Prinz Lorenz arena to see Django. We'd talked about getting a hotel room first. But both of us were too hyped up for that. So we asked directions and went straight to the arena.

It had none of the Maxima's ancient majesty, looking more like a vast concrete fortress than a place where great music happened. The streets around it were more crowded, dirtier, and louder. The Guardia there were called Polizei. They wore coal black uniforms with Northland runic emblems. Some had riot helmets and shock batons. Lined up in squads, glaring at the swelling mob, they looked like soldiers about to attack.

Above the arena was a huge billboard advertising the show. "Last Time Ever!" the crimson letters shouted. "Django Conn's final show!" Below that was a massive picture of Django, grand as the Emperor of Dimension X. They'd even given him a scepter and a crown. *Last time? Final show?*

"Do you think it's true?" I asked Anna Z. "Or just hype? Is it really the final show?"

She shrugged, looking confused and maybe even a little afraid. She didn't know any more than me. It was all foreign here: the look of the people, their accents, the cold stone architecture, the rules and laws, the way the Polizei shoved the crowd and shouted orders. There was even a squad on horseback, like cavalry brought in to herd the peasants this way and that. We got into the line, and it was a very good thing we'd skipped going to the hotel, as it took three hours to get our tickets.

SEVENTY-NINE

The feel that day was different than at the Maxima. Everyone seemed on edge, ready to go crazy, seething with excitement. Plenty of kids were glammed-up, dressed in full moonglow glister. Hair was dyed every color of the spectrum, and a few I'd never seen. Even though the Polizei were out in full force, fashion ruled. Boys with platform heels, skintight jumpsuits, heavy necklaces of turquoise and amber. Girls in feathers and furs, silver capes, golden robes. It was all there hours before the doors opened.

The rhythm of the voices, a rougher feel to the way people talked, made me feel like a foreigner. I listened in to the kids around us. Just a hundred miles away, and even the slang here was different. The band was "sprooly" and the new record "razz." I heard one kid said he was ready to "drill and spill," whatever that meant. A couple of ticket scalpers had already been beaten up and robbed of their precious goods. Everybody was hyped for Django, of course, fanatics like me and Anna Z. But the stakes seemed higher here than at the Maxima. Maybe this really was Django's last show. Maybe it would be a party and a funeral blast, a wild celebration for his last goodbye.

I asked a kid with a blue and orange comet painted on his face if this was the final show of the tour, or forever. He laughed, screwed up his eyes, and yelled over the crowd's din, "Luigi!"

"What?" I yelled back.

He made two fists and beat them in the air. "Luigi!" Then I realized who it was—the weird kid I'd seen the day before at the record store.

"Hey, you came all the way here too!" he said. "This is going to be madness. You listening? *Absolute madness.* You ready for that?" Getting only a shrug from me, he looked at Anna Z and said, "You ready? This is the end. The end of the end of the end. Everything and anything can happen." He grabbed her, pulled her close, trying to kiss her. She squirmed away, and he laughed it off. "See you on the astral plane!" he yelled and went shoving his way toward the front of the crowd.

The doors opened an hour before Django was supposed to hit the stage. The crowd at the Maxima had been wild and excited. Here, it was totally out of control. Already there were fights, high-fashion girls getting mauled by gangs of bruiser-boys, kids hitting the white gong too hard, too soon. The Polizei didn't even try to keep order now, drawing back, giving up. With a roar and a shrilling wail, ten thousand kids surged into the arena. I grabbed for Anna Z, like we were in a whirlpool in a black-storm ocean. I got her shoulder, then yanked myself nearer and took hold of her hand. The whirlpool poured into a gaping entrance, and we went with it like little bits of driftwood.

EIGHTY

The Prinz Lorenz arena was much bigger than the Maxima.
The ceiling was a vast dome, supported by iron arches. There
were bleacher seats on three sides, facing the stage. And
some kids were heading that way. We went with the real
fans, down to the main floor. Slowly, still hand in hand,
we wormed our way closer to the stage. Everyone on the
floor wanted to be up front too, of course. Some worked
their way toward the middle of the stage, where Django
would appear. Others pushed toward the stacks of speakers,
which stood like huge black monoliths on the right and left.

Music came from the PA system, something by Corelli
I think, but amped-up and drum-driven. The sound wasn't
good, all that concrete above us making a boomy echo. I
tried to say something to Anna Z. She just shrugged and
shook her head. I pulled her closer, and yelled into her
ear, "I'm happy!" Just a couple of words. She kissed me on
the cheek and yelled back something that might've had
the word "love" in it. But it got swept away in a hysterical
shout from the crowd.

The stage lights started flashing squid-scarlet and rep-
tile-green. The big Django logo above the stage came to

life, a comet burning through the night sky. A blast of synthetic horns buried the Corelli. Adrenaline seethed in my veins and in the crowd too. I could feel it coming in sizzling waves. The logo started to spin, slow at first. Crimson became fiery brightness. Green flared into a blue-hot metallic sheen. An announcer was yelling about Django. The crowd was yelling a thousand times louder, sweeping him away. I think I heard the words "last time ever." A girl next to me was already crying, hyped to hysteria. I looked at Anna Z and got a shimmering glimpse of the light on her glasses. And then the band was on stage, blasting into "That Alien Feel."

EIGHTY-ONE

It was just the band at first: Rudy on gamba, Simon on baryton, Mick on drums. They made the royal shining noise, the riff-riot fanfare. A flaming pink spotlight showed us where Django would appear. Twenty thousand eyes were aimed at that incandescent circle. One moment it was empty, and then Django was there before us. If the crowd was wild before, now it was berserk, shoving and grabbing, desperate to get nearer. I added my scream to the massive scream, and it was like I was yelling through ten thousand mouths. Anna Z screamed too, though I couldn't separate her voice from the nerve-smashing din. We screamed as one, Django held his arms over his head like a priest giving his blessing, and the lyrics to "That Alien Feel" swept over us.

Django had a different look than at the Maxima. It took me a song or two to calm down and notice the change. He was thinner, paler, and his costume showed off more skin. His hair was full of shiny spikes and greasy corkscrews. Even his expressions—what little I could see of his face— made me think that he'd given up something. The band was louder than at the Maxima, the bass-end throb punching my heart and the treble-shriek clawing at my skull. Django's voice had all the power and laser-bright feeling of before. He moved on the stage like the Last King of the Universe. Still, what hit me was how exposed he was, open to our eyes and ears and grasping hands. This wasn't weakness but a kind of strength, I think, as if he had nothing to lose and so nothing could hurt him.

The band hit the last chord of "X-Ray Spex" and without dropping a beat went into "I Fear No Venom." I sang along with Django, knowing the song by heart. And when we got to the chorus, it was as though my voice was booming out through the PA system.

> *I fear no venom*
> *I fear no sting*
> *I fear no poison*
> *not anything.*

Rudy took a solo, heavy with distortion, while Django came up right to the edge of the stage. Kids were reaching for him, frantic. He was reaching down to them, cool and white as December moonlight. Anna Z pushed forward. I lost my hold on her, and it was like panic turned itself into sound: buzzing, throbbing, pounding inside my skull. I fought my way toward Anna Z, and that was when I saw Lukas.

EIGHTY-TWO

Just a flash, a ghost—the face of Anna Z's brother far off in the swirling sea of kids. A wave of sick feeling broke over me, and now I knew how it would all end. Of course Lukas had read about Django's last show. Of course he'd known that Anna Z would have to go there. And of course he'd come to find her and take her back, forever. I got a far away glimpse of him, dark as the Duke of Doomsville, and I could see the end of it all: Anna Z gone. Me alone.

But the spectral Lukas disappeared as Django sang out, "You're not alone!" The band had gone dead for just those few seconds, and Django's voice filled the entire arena. I was sure those words were for Anna Z and me. Had I really seen Lukas? Maybe. Had Django pointed down to us and wailed, "You're not alone!" Absolutely.

I lunged between two kids and got hold of Anna Z. Somebody shoved me, hard, and I lost her again. Fingernails raked down the side of my face. Another kid went down, and it seemed like the others around him just trampled over him. I wasn't the only one who thought the words were for me. At the edge of the stage, the crowd was so densely packed that it would've taken a hammer and a chisel to break through the bodies. They swayed together like a huge sea creature with countless arms. Hands waved and fingers clawed at the air. Ten thousand kids around me, and I *was* alone, unless I got to her again.

> *I fear no venom*
> *I fear no sting*
> *I fear no poison*
> *not anything.*

Django wailed it and I sang along, hoarse and gasping. But of course, it wasn't true. I was full of fear, almost choking on it. Panic-sweat, the cloud of fly-spell smoke, stinging perfumes, and maybe even my own blood: the smell was awful. Every breath was like sucking in the exhaust from an over-stoked furnace.

The lights from above hit us, and I saw in Anna Z's face the same look I'd seen at the Maxima. She was gone, gone, maximum gone. She'd given up everything, and that included me. Her name, where she'd come from, and where she was going, all she'd done with me in the last days: they vanished in that moment.

In movies, I'd heard wild jungle cats screaming at night to find their mates or just because there's all that tropical hunger vibe in them. And howler monkeys and weird birds too, all blue and purple with spikes of feathers like horns. Blasts of jungle primitivo noise in the flickering darkness. And that's what I heard that night at the arena. I know it was just a band: drums, gamba, baryton, and Django Conn at the mic. I know it was just a mob of star-crazed kids.

But there was something else happening too: jungle cat attack screams, bizarre insects buzzing, and shimmering tentacles wrapped around our brains.

EIGHTY-THREE

Maybe it didn't matter that her brother was there, moving in toward her. Maybe every single minute she'd spent with me was just to get her here, totally gone. The first time I saw her this way, it was amazing. Now it was amazing and heartbreaking. Pure wild escape into the power, and sadness like a tidal wave. There was no way to separate them: To gain, she had to lose. To get filled up, she had to be emptied out first. Maybe it didn't matter that Lukas had come there to claim her back. She'd gotten what she most wanted, and she'd known all along the price she'd have to pay.

I stopped trying to reach her. As long as I didn't lose sight, I had what I wanted. Just to see Anna Z was enough. Her face was empty as clear glass. And it was full too. It shone like a mirror reflecting the alien light. Above, beyond, and forever—the electrum skies shining inside and out. That's what I'd seen at the Maxima. That was the real, true, perfect Anna Z.

With four huge quaking chords, the band came to a halt. Django waited, taking a couple of deep breaths, then said he wanted us all to be quiet. Ten thousand kids yelled back, louder. He was serious though. He called out again for us to really listen. Back and forth it went, but each time the crowd got quieter.

Finally, Django got what he asked for. He took a couple of deep breaths before announcing, "This isn't just the last show of the tour. This is the last one I'll ever do with the Reptiles. It's been beautiful. I love the band. But this is the end." The crowd screamed and surged at the stage. He waited until we were quiet again and said they were going to do a new song called "Meet Me in the Strange." The whole arena was silent as Django wrapped a filmy robe around himself. It was almost see-through, and as he turned slowly, it billowed out to make a glimmering cloud around him.

Rudy's gamba sounded first, a riff made of gold and silver, tearing a hole in the darkness. Then the baryton and drums came in, coppery strings and iron hammers. And when Django sang the chorus of the song, his voice was pure mercury.

> *Meet me in the strange*
> *—secret places!*
> *Meet me in the strange*
> *—secret faces!*
> *Meet me in the strange*
> *—secret seeming!*
> *Meet me in the strange*
> *—secret gleaming!*
> *Meet me in the strange*
> *and you'll never be alone.*

EIGHTY-FOUR

Alone or not, Lukas found her. The crowd parted as he came toward the stage. Dressed in a somber black suit, he was obviously not one of Django's devoted fans. He didn't need to push very much. Kids drew back, feeling the menace in him as much as they saw how unlike them he was.

I heard Lukas call out to Anna Z. He made her name into a wail of pure pain and loss. That his voice could be heard over the band seemed impossible. Still, his sister's name cut through the din from on stage. I was yelling it too, a warning thrown like a tiny pebble into a storm-swollen sea.

She was too far from me to reach, and too far into the music to save, even if I could've grabbed her and dragged her out of the arena. Even if I'd been the shining knight and had some heroic plan to get rid of her brother. Even if I'd been Frankenstein's creature, strong as twenty men. No one could save Anna Z except herself.

Now she was right at the edge of the stage. Django was singing about someone meeting him "in the strange," holding the mic stand with both hands as though he'd fall over without its support. Lukas pushed by me, blind to everything but his sister. He punched a girl, and she went down screaming. He kicked a guy hard, like he was breaking down a door. His voice really did reach me now, calling to Anna Z with all the power of a cracking bullwhip.

He came at Anna Z, grabbing for her. Hemmed in by the crowd, there was only one direction for her to go—straight ahead. As Django spun in his cloudy glimmer-robe, as he tottered, eyes closed and head tilted back for his final cry, Anna Z made it to the stage and climbed up. Security men emerged, like bats flying out of a cave to whisk her away. But Django straightened up, having gotten at last to the end of the song, and strength returned to his body. He waved the guards away and reached to take Anna Z's hand.

EIGHTY-FIVE

It was rare, but sometimes fans made it onto the stage. Once in a while, a singer will let a girl stand beside him for a few seconds, let her kiss him or give him her offering of flowers, and then have his security men usher her away. On either side of the arena's stage were caves of curtained darkness. That's where the girls went, off to instant oblivion. Some bands had stage groupies, and they got special treatment, I suppose. Mostly though, they had their second or two in the spotlight and disappeared.

This was different and everybody knew it. Ten thousand kids watched as Django took Anna Z's hand and pulled her into the cloud that surrounded him: strobing spotlights, shimmering fabric, dry ice fog, concert-buzz. Her glasses gleamed and the look on her face was pure joy. Django spoke into the mic, saying that the show was over, the tour was over, the band was over. He raised his hands over his head, shouted a last goodbye to his fans, and vanished with Anna Z into the dark nothing.

While this went on, her brother was still trying to get onto the stage. He had no chance. Though his grief made Lukas strong and wild as a killer shark, the security guys knew how to handle him. With shock batons and a lot of muscle, they kept Anna Z's brother away from the band. Mick got up from the drum set and fled. As Rudy and Simon put down their instruments, the last wave of fan-madness crushed against the stage. At the head of this surge, Lukas threw himself against the wall of guards. The wall held.

Later, the TV reporters said there'd been a riot at the arena. But I don't think "riot" is the right word. It got insane, that much is true. People got hurt, though nobody died. The Polizei did come in with fire hoses at the end, to flush the last of the fans away. I saw some blood, and I heard a lot of screaming. But a riot seems to me a bad thing, a lot of pent-up rage and wanting to destroy. None of the kids I saw that night were angry. Nobody except Lukas wanted to hurt anyone else. It was just the last wave of excitement from the show, the buzz of seeing Django, and a lot of straight-up sadness that pushed the fans to go wild that night. He said it was the last show and we believed him. We'd been so close, we could see the sweat on his face, and now we might never see him in person again. That's what made the kids so crazy.

Pushed all the way to the front, I tried a couple of times to climb on the stage, to follow Anna Z. But the moment for that was long gone. She'd found the perfect time to break the invisible wall. She'd gone through and it closed up behind her. The arena's overhead lights came on, cold and empty-bright. The security guys swung their batons, shoved and yelled for us to back off. The Polizei, with riot shields and helmets, appeared on either side of the stage.

They came at us in two wedge-shaped squadrons, and we were pushed back, back, back.

EIGHTY-SIX

I was still on the street outside the arena two hours later. Steel gates had been pulled across all the entrances. The doors were closed and locked. No lights shone in the windows far overhead. Only the craziest and the truest of the true believers were left. Django had left the arena long before. Why were we here? The others, the sad, broken-looking kids, had no other place to be. This was the spot they'd been dreaming about for weeks, the most important place on the planet. Now it was just a huge, ugly concrete fortress. An empty shell. Still, inside they'd seen the real thing, the last of Django and the Albino Reptiles from Dimension X. It was like they'd been to a gigantic bonfire and were hanging around to catch the faint glow of the last embers.

That's not why I stayed. I kept thinking one of the big steel gates would open and out Anna Z would come. And if that happened, I had to be there. How else would we find each other again? We hadn't talked about what to do if we got separated. It didn't even seem possible the night before. We were together, we were going to Django, and that had been everything.

The other kids drifted away one by one. A girl came clomping down the empty sidewalk. One of her platform heels had broken off, and she walked with a sideways, twisting limp. As she passed, I saw her makeup was streaked with dried tears. I was going to ask her something, anything, but she shook her head, as though to say she couldn't help me. A boy with sky-blue hair followed her, a few paces behind. He didn't even look at me.

EIGHTY-SEVEN

Anna Z had gone to Django. I'd lost her. And gone is really gone, I kept telling myself. Dead or just vanished. Never to be seen again. Off to the other side of the world or to the family mausoleum. What difference did it make? Gone is gone. On an airplane that will never come back or a spaceship to the moon. In a coffin or a rocket. If it was true that I'd never see her again, then traveling is the same thing as being dead. No letters would come from where Anna Z had gone. She wasn't going to pick up the phone and tell me about her new life in the New World.

That's what I kept thinking as I wandered around outside the dead, empty arena. I'd be here, forever. And she was *there*, somewhere, in a place with no name.

But at least she was safe now. That thought gave me some comfort. She was free from her brother. I couldn't protect her from him. But surely with Django Conn, in the court of the Glister King, she'd be all right. I could picture her with all the others there: boys and girls in the wildest fashion finery, musicians from around the world, big names, beautiful celebrities. As long as she stayed there, Django's people would keep her safe. He'd have guards at his court, like any king. There was no way they'd let Lukas come and take her away.

My mind kept going there, imagining Anna Z and her new, freer, happier life. I wandered the block like a lost soul, lost in my own mind. I went to the news dealer—the only thing open at that hour—and looked at the big racks of magazines. Dozens of glamorous faces smiled back at me. Film and TV stars, singers and drummers and gamba-gods, Apollonauts in their gleaming suits, the now famous and the soon-to-be. I thought that someday I'd see Anna Z's face on one of those magazine covers. She'd be there, *Homo lux*, a gorgeous creature made of light and sound.

EIGHTY-EIGHT

Everything hurt. My feet from being stepped on, my legs from standing all night, my face from being scratched, my throat from shouting until I was hoarse. And of course the worst hurt wasn't in my body. For a short time, a couple of days, I'd had everything I ever wanted. And now she was gone.

I had to accept what was obviously true. Anna Z wasn't coming out of the arena. She probably hadn't been in there since the band took off. The entourage had slipped out the back while the riot was going on. That's how it always worked: the band was gone before the fans had been cleared out. By this time, Anna Z could've been hundreds of miles away.

In the train station, I looked at posters for mountaintop resorts, Alpine castles, ocean beaches, the greatest museums and concert halls on the continent. Now, I told myself, I could travel to any place I wanted. I could spend the rest of my life wandering. When my cash ran out, I was sure my father would send more by wire. He wouldn't like it. He might send one of Hermann's men to try to get me to come home. But there was no way he'd let me starve in a faraway city. I seriously thought about going. Anywhere. Everywhere. Why not? What did I have to lose?

"You still here?" The voice broke me out of my daze, too loud for this empty street.

I looked up. It was the kid with the comet painted on his face, the one from Luigi's.

EIGHTY-NINE

"You know where the party is?"

"What party?" I asked

"Stupido," he said. "Maximum stupido. You coming or not? I just found out which hotel it's at. Come on, come on, come on." He said this in one quick, rattling burst. "Everybody who's anybody is there. The band, the insiders, the press, the right fans. That's you and me, okay? True believers and some white gong. Friend or foe, yes or no? Let's go, let's go, let's go."

"Is Django still here?" I asked.

"Not here. At the hotel. It isn't far. I've been asking for an hour, and I just got the word. I had to pass along a little of the good stuff, but it's worth it. You can always get more, right? The party's still going strong. At the Mount Moritz. It'll keep cooking till daybreak. Got it? Now let's go. It's time to party." The first time I'd met him, the kid had seemed a bit depresso. Before the show, outside the arena, he'd been manic. Now, with the blue and orange comet melting on his face, draggled clothes and nonstop chatter, he seemed like something out of a comic book. He didn't tell me his name or ask me mine.

To me, he was just Comet Boy, my guide, my info, and my in.

"It's amazing," he said. "I heard that Django's still there, and all the guys from the band. There's some movie people, and that writer from Creedo, the one with the—"

"T.V. Geist?"

"Yeah. That's him. And about five hundred girls and a pile of primo fly-spell taller than you or me and it's happening right now."

"But how are we going to get in?"

"Just stick with me, Stupido. I'm the fan with the plan. And I'll do what I can."

NINETY

The Mount Moritz was the fanciest hotel in the city. Not as big as the Angelus, not as old or as beautiful, but still it had what some people would call grandeur. It had a golden glow, like a castle that had just floated down from heaven. I was used to walking right into the Angelus, so I headed for the main lobby.

"Hang on," Comet Boy said, grabbing my arm. "You think they're going to let you just waltz in? I found out about a side entrance. For the cooks and maids. We can get in there, and then I do my magic." He pulled out a plastic bag full of crystalline white powder. "Nobody says no to a pinch of this. If God made anything better, he kept it for himself."

We went around the side of the hotel, down a narrower street, but I kept asking myself, *What are you doing?* Even if we got in, even if we got to the party, what was the point? Anna Z had found what she wanted. She'd gone to Django, and he'd accepted her, taken her up on the stage and whisked her away. She didn't want me anymore. She'd gotten what she'd come for.

But Comet Boy had a kind of wild gravity about him,

pulling me along. He was so up, so sure of himself that I didn't argue.

He was right. There was a side entrance. A gaggle of glammed-up girls—they had to be younger than me—were hanging around there, trying to get past the guy at the desk. They laughed and flirted and pleaded in singsongy voices. Finally he pointed to one of the girls, who was showing more skin than the rest. She went to him, he grabbed her around the waist, and that was our chance. Comet Boy gave me a hard elbow in the side, and we zipped by the desk.

NINETY-ONE

The feel there was different than any place at the Angelus, or at least it was that night. We ran down the hall, like invaders who'd gotten past the first line of enemy defense. An elevator opened and spilled out twice as many people as it should have held. We climbed over a guy who was obviously way gone on something illegal, and I pounded the button to shut the doors.

So we got to the twelfth floor without anybody telling us to leave. There were people everywhere, some of them drunk, some zoned on who-knows-what, some just hyped on the post-gig party energy.

"Where do you think he is?" Comet Boy said. "He's here somewhere. I can feel it. But which room, which room, which room?"

I didn't have any idea about that. This was all new to me, all too much already. Maybe Django really was there, but more importantly, Anna Z was too. I might not get her back. I knew the odds of that were tiny. There was no way she'd give up this—being in the court of the Glister King—for what she had before. But I thought if I could just see her one more time, to really say goodbye, it would be okay for me to go home to the Angelus and my old life.

"Where is he?" Comet Boy asked a girl who'd come tumbling out of a room. "Is he in there?"

She just laughed and started pounding on the door, which somebody had slammed behind her.

"Where's the main party? Where's Django?" Comet Boy had his bag of white crystals out now, dangling it like a lantern to light his way in darkness. "I got the goods. Come on, come on, come on, somebody tell me where he is!"

This was a big mistake. A security guy, who probably weighed more than the both of us put together, saw what Comet Boy was doing and came down on him like a hammer. Luckily by then, the crowd had pushed us apart somewhat. The security guy grabbed Comet Boy, dragged him into a room, and I was alone again.

NINETY-TWO

Now what? I asked myself, standing in the hallway as knots of people tangled around me. What did I have that would get me what I wanted?

A door crashed open, and I got a glimpse of a much bigger space. Yelling, laughter, music, a hundred hyped conversations blurring into one surge of noise. It was the main party room. It had to be.

Maybe pharmaceuticals wouldn't work, but I still had my wad of money. I pulled it out, started peeling off bank notes and headed for the door. A guy who had to be three heads taller than me stood guard. He said, "Put it away, kid. Somebody'll grab it." Then he turned to say hi to somebody and I was in.

A squad of fan-girls had shimmied down from the floor above and gotten to a balcony window. Django's roadies were drinking, blowing off steam, and when they saw all those girl-faces and girl-bodies pressed up against the glass, they went a bit mad. Somebody with a movie camera was already there, setting up his lights and sound equipment as though it was a film set. I just stood off to the side there for a little while, watching, soaking in the craziness. Freaks and fakes, players from other bands, a gypsy fortune-teller, a fire-eater from the circus, and an Indian snake-dancer had showed up too.

Some older guys were near me. Listening, I figured out there were studio techs, talking about Django's next record. And I even got a glimpse of T.V. Geist, the writer from Creedo. He was skinny, very pale, with his bulby head shaved clean and a goat-beard waggling on his chin. His voice was louder than most, and sharper, cutting through the din. "You really want to know? Get a bucket and a mop right now, because this'll blow your brain. I'm serious as a shark-bite. This one will melt you down to a puddle of blue goo."

I edged closer, trying to hear the secret he was threatening to reveal. It wouldn't be about Anna Z, I understood that. But because he was famous, and could get the inside story, I thought maybe he knew if Django was still there at the hotel.

It didn't happen that way. We never met. I was close enough to hear the wheeze in T.V.'s voice between the words. But before I asked him the big question, there came a scream, a slam and a string of curses from the doorway.

Lukas had found the party and was there to get his sister back.

NINETY-THREE

It got insane very fast. Lukas had already been knocked around, probably fighting with the Polizei at the arena. One of his sleeves was ripped, and his left eye was swollen almost shut. He'd been a madman before. Now he was a doom-rocket, blasting straight for his target.

One of the roadies tried to toss him out and was soon down on the floor with blood all over his face. Kids were running around now and the movie guy was trying to get it on film. The snake dancer started wailing in a weird, inhuman voice. More roadies went into action. And though they were big, tough, and used to dealing with unruly fans, Lukas had a ball of burning hate inside his heart. And he had nothing to lose anymore.

He picked up a chair and swung it around his head, keeping everybody back. "Where is she?" he screamed. "I want her back!"

Somebody told him to cool it, and he threw the chair. Before anyone could get him though, he'd picked up another one. "I'll kill everyone in the room if I have to. I'll do it. Now tell me where she is."

"Who?"

That made him even madder. "You want to die right now?" he shrieked. "I'll kill you all."

Then a door opened at the back of the room. And there was Django Conn: calm and silent. He almost glowed, that's what it seemed like, with a cold, imperial, alien power. Anna Z was beside him, like his young queen. I yelled out her name. She turned toward me. Lukas turned too, for just a second, and then lunged straight at Django, filled to overflowing with that freak-out energy.

Someone must've called the Polizei as soon as he'd gotten into the Mount Moritz. Because four of them, armed riot-troopers, stormed into the hotel room just as Lukas made his last attack. He fought back, and it was a good thing they hadn't sent only one. It was ugly, and wild, and it hurt me to watch it. Lukas might've been wrong-wrong-wrong for Anna Z. He'd messed with her in ways nobody ever should. But it was loss and grief that drove him now, the pure misery of losing her forever.

As the Polizei brought him down, he kept yelling that Anna Z belonged to him and nobody else. She was his and his only. How could she do this to him?

Assaulting a roadie was bad enough, fighting back against a law officer in that city—and breaking bones—meant there was definitely jail ahead for Anna Z's brother. A long stretch of hard time. They dragged him out, cuffed at the wrists and ankles.

Anna Z looked up into Django's eyes. He didn't smile or nod, but there was a big yes in the look he gave her. She crossed the room, the crowd parting for her, and she said, "This is Davi."

NINETY-FOUR

"It's perfect. Nobody'll bother us down here." We'd found two seats together at the back of a car. The sun was just coming up as the train came out of the tunnel. "We'll be home in a couple of hours, and I need to tell you everything before we get there. Okay? So just listen. You're the best listener in the world, Davi. And I need that now more than anything.

"Just listen and try to understand. 'It was the secrets of heaven and earth that I desired to learn.' Doctor Franken-stein said that. I read those words when I was little, and I never forgot them. It was like he was talking straight to me. That's what the story is really about and what the creature is really made out of. Not dead body parts and chemicals but the secrets of heaven and earth. That's why we went to the show, right? And that's why you found me and I found you and we went to Django together. To meet me in the strange and find out the secrets of heaven and earth."

We sat together in our secret place, a pair of seats that faced backward, set off from the others by an overloaded luggage compartment. With her arm around my shoulder, holding me tight, she talk-talk-talked. Her breath was warm in my ear. Her hand felt hot, squeezing mine. Her face was flushed, as though a fever was rising inside her.

"I'm still a virgin, if that's what you're wondering. You and me, Davi, the last virgins. I did get to be with Django for a little while, just the two of us. He didn't need another girl. Not for that. He's got a million, if he wants them. And they're all willing. That's not why he let me come up on stage and then go with him back to the party. He wanted to talk to me, and when I told him about you, he said you could come around some time too. And he really meant it. He's even more amazing in person, I mean one-on-one, than in concert. I could feel the weird vibe coming off him like the pure energy of a star. A real star, massive solar, like the sun: light and heat and something else I don't think there's even a word for.

"We just talked. Me and Django. That's all. We talked about his songs a little, and what we've both seen in the skies, and how everybody is an alien. That's what he explained. We really are all aliens. It's just that some of us feel it deeper. You and me get it the way most people don't. We all come from Dimension X. Or the dark side of the moon. Alpha Centuri, Albebaran, or Arcturus. Doesn't matter what name you use, it's still *out there*. It's still *The Strange*. It's where we come from and where we're going. 'Meet me in the strange secret faces.' That's what Django was talking about in that song. You and me look up at the sky and we see the electrum light. Everybody could too if they looked. Everybody wants it but they just don't know how to get it."

NINETY-FIVE

It came out like a storm. A first wave, a whirlwind, then a lull, and another blast of words. It came in a brilliant swirl and muddy jumble. The facts, the feelings, what she saw, what she heard, what Django said. Secrets of heaven and earth? Maybe. Sights and sounds she'd never experienced before? I think so. Did she meet somebody in the strange? Absolutely.

"Django said that everybody wants it bad. Like the people who stand in line, all the way around the block for hours, just to be the first into a theater to see a new movie. They could wait a few days, right? And there'd be no lines then. But people want to get there the first day because there's something in the pictures and the voices, in the light and the sound, something that people call magic, but that's not the right word. They want to be in that first wave of The Strange when it comes off the screen and out of the speakers.

"Or like the people at the cathedral with their saints and statues and beads. They believe and it really matters. They pray and sing and bow down. They've got the idea that somewhere in the cathedral, there's power and glory, and if they do the right things, they might get a little taste of it. And you know what, Davi? We're not much different really. You and me going to Django are like the old ladies who go on a pilgrimage to their special shrines and holy wells. And they come back different. Going to the show was our pilgrimage. We went and now we're going back, changed forever."

NINETY-SIX

New movies and old pilgrims, true believers and The Strange: those were important. I got that. But was that really why she was there with me, going home, instead of traveling with Django? If he was so amazing and he chose her out of all those thousands of girls to come up on stage, then why would she *choose me?* What possible reason could she have for giving up the new Star-World, the court of the great Glister King, for the old Angelus and little me?

"He needs us here, Davi. That's what he told me. Bright virgin specters. And if it's not you and me, then who? Was there anybody at the Maxima who really got him and his music the way we did? No, no, and Triple-X No. We're it. We're his Flash Bang Babies: 'I'll be your ears. I'll be your eyes.' That's what he really needs, for us to stay where we really live and keep watching the skies. That's where it's really going to happen. More music and mutation? Listening deeper into his sound? Opening up to the Alien Drift? Yes, yes, and Triple-Y Yes. But there's a place for us, and it's not wandering around the New World with the band.

"He's going to do an album in the New World. Something fresh. A whole new sound with new musicians to work with. He already has a new name for the band: the Alien Drifters. Sort of an outer space cowboy vibe. The plan is to move there, to the New World, and make a record that will change everything. Break it all wide open. It's supposed to take six months. I heard people saying that's how much time he's booked at the studio. Maybe more. On the other side of the world. It's going to be a different sound, a different feel, way past everything he's done before."

He was taking his whole entourage to the New World, and she could've gone along. For a few weeks, it might be wondrous. That was the word she kept using, "wondrous." Traveling with his people would be like nothing she'd ever seen or felt. And he told her it was up to her to choose. But she didn't play any instruments and she hardly sang. What good would she do him there? After a while, she'd just be one more girl. Maybe a wondrous, wild girl, but still, just another Django-mad fan. She didn't just want to follow the band around like a groupie. There was a more important job for her to do.

When he made his Grand Comeback, when the album was done and he did the world tour with his new band and sound, then we'd be here, ready. He needed our ears and eyes. That's what he told her. He needed his young spectral virgins. He'd be back, in a year or two, and when he came through on the tour, we could be with him again.

NINETY-SEVEN

"He told me to stay free. That was the most important part. If I went with the band, it would be wondrous, weird, and good. But he said that after a while it would have to end. He's amazing, Davi. He sees something for just a few seconds and he gets it, like he's been studying it for weeks.

"Lukas is gone, gone, gone. Off to jail. And I'm really free. That was what Django saw right away. We heard the fight, the yelling, and I knew right off that it was Lukas. Django took my hand. It was the only time he touched me at the party. He just held my hand and said everything was going to be all right. We went out to the big room and that's when Django really got it. He saw the whole thing in a flash.

"I need to be free, and if I went with the band, no matter how amazing it might be for me, still I'd lose something. I wouldn't be free anymore. And that's why I'm back, Davi. That's why I'm with you. For the first time in my life, I'm free. When we get back, we'll have the whole city for ourselves, and we won't have to sneak around. No more running away, hiding, being afraid all the time.

"Django got it. He understood me and my brother, and

you too, even though you've never really met him yet. It was like he saw right inside me and knew everything. So we're going back where we belong. It'll be the same, sort of, and totally different too. I know it, Davi. I feel it. I'm free. And so are you. Really free."

NINETY-EIGHT

That night, Anna Z went back to our rooftop. And I followed. She stood for me there clothed in a shimmering cloud. Her body, pale as alien sky-gleam, shone through the haze of Django's robe, the one he'd worn for the last song. Her wild hair framed her face like a black halo. She stood there with her arms out, her hands upraised, as though she could catch the moonlight like drops of rain.

The night sky was huge, and the city too, bigger than it had ever been before. The city glimmered all around us, ten thousand lights, ten thousand fragments of crushed jewels catching the light of the moon. Everything had changed since we'd been away. Only one day and the city seemed to have spread, stretched, grown brighter and more alive. Of course, it wasn't the city that had mutated overnight. It was me—my eyes and ears and tongue—that had changed. The meal we ate, down in the east kitchen with Maria-Claire, was stronger and better than any I'd ever had. The nerves of my skin seemed to feel what they couldn't before: a glittering knife edge, the sleekness of a crimson silk shirt I put on after taking a long bath, the smooth warmth of the rooftop's tarred surface. Even the night air tasted different: a clean, pure blackness.

What happened that night on the rooftop was impossible, but I don't care anymore what can be true and what can't. All I care about now is what I saw and heard and felt. The bells of St. Florian's were ringing, and I heard Django's music in the tolling. The whole band echoed in the far-off midnight bell-peal: gamba and baryton and drums. Mostly though, it was Django's voice crying out, sleek and bright as mercury, from the top of the cathedral tower.

> *Meet me in the strange*
> *and you'll never be alone.*

The first word I ever heard Anna Z say was "impossible." I'd been crouching alone in darkness. I'd been hiding, listening in on Sabina's séance, and I'd heard the word but didn't know who was talking. "Impossible" is what people say when their minds are too small to hold a huge idea or a bizarre dream or something they know is true but it makes them feel crazy.

I felt crazy now, and bizarre and huge. But it was the good kind of crazy. Confused too. Of course I was mixed-up, crazy with joy—like I was asleep and waking at the same time—seeing Anna Z that way before me.

A slow storm—that's the best way I can describe it. Not special effects slo-mo like in a movie, but a storm happening outside of time. Maybe gravity was different that night. Or maybe gravity doesn't even touch light and sound and time. I don't have the science to explain it, and even if I did, I'd probably just stick with what Anna Z and I called it later. The slow storm. Power and glory, for sure. Huge, wondrous streaks of light across the sky. The sound of the cathedral bells turned into liquid metal spirit-spears. And passing through us, both of us. Falling without gravity, moving through our bodies and leaving behind the secret forever feel.

The storm fell and I swear on the Virgin Mary Shelley *we rose*. I don't mean that we went zooming into the sky. But there was definitely levitation going on. We rose and the sky opened, welcoming us. Anna Z spun round in Django's robe. I watched, and though my body stayed put, my mind was spinning too, in luminous spirals. We were truly specters that night, our bodies turning into heaven-gleam and the tolling of the uppermost bells. We rose, together, blurring into each other, filling each other, and filling the sky above.

NINETY-NINE

Two weeks later, Django was on the cover of *Creedo*. The picture showed him on stage at the Prinz Lorenz arena. Though I'd been there, the camera caught something in Django that I hadn't seen. Maybe it was just the distance, the angle, the colors. Maybe they'd messed with the picture for the cover. But Django looked almost see-through. The shot was from the very end of the show, with him in that weird robe that Anna Z brought back with her. I suppose it was just the shimmery material of the robe, and not his actual body that gave that transparent feel. Either way, holding the mag in my hands and staring at the cover, I wondered what else I *hadn't seen* at the show.

The robe was gone. I'd seen Anna Z in it the night of the slow storm. The robe, the gleams of light, her body, and nothing else. The next day she'd hidden it away somewhere in the Angelus, telling me that it was for later. When Django came back on his next world tour, then I'd see it, I'd see her in it again.

The cover story was by T.V. Geist, and I read it out loud to Anna Z as soon as I got it back to my room. We lay on the bed together, not really touching but close enough to feel each other's body heat. Or astral vibes, alpha waves, solar soul rays: whatever you want to call it.

Anna Z had her eyes closed. She liked it when I read to her. The day after we got back from the show, I found some books she remembered from when she was younger. *The Outermost Stars, The Phantom Phace of Phaethon, The Girl-Queen of Mars.* She said it made her feel safe, like a little kid, when I read to her. I asked her if I should try to imitate T.V. Geist's voice. She told me, "It doesn't matter. Just read it the way it feels right to you." His words, my voice.

ONE HUNDRED

"How many times can Django Conn reinvent himself? How many fingers you got, honey? How many toes? Fan-girls say he's sexy as a midnight tomcat, but I'm here to tell you that he's got way more than nine sweet, secret lives. Maybe *reincarnation* is a better word for what this gilt-edged glam guru has managed again.

"He died last night, sort of, and came back to life, sort-of-kind-of. If you're a true believer in the Django-jingo, if you're reading these words, which I guess you must be, then you already know about the so-called Righteous Riot at the Prinz Lorenz. I was there, and I survived. I've seen real post-show pandemonium, and this was more like a movie-mogul's idea of a riot than the genuine thing. Still, people got pretty riled, and the Polizei came down with their iron-heeled boots. Hard and heavy.

· "So what? So this: Django kind of died while the riot was supposedly going on. A brand new song, a blast of x-rays, a goodbye, and he died. I was backstage. I saw him vanish—poof!—like a Ghost From the Coast. There was a girl, I think, with him (glasses, crazy black hair, you out there?) and she vanished with him. Maybe she's the new

Lady Conn. Or maybe she's just part of the con-game too (he did change his name to Conn for a reason, folks). I don't know. All I've got to work with is this brain and this tongue. So here's my big thinks and my big words. Here's the prediction: Django Conn is a transformer and the high-voltage mutation power is zapping through him. He will indeed come back, but you may not recognize him.

"After he died and came back again, I got about thirty-three and a third seconds with the Mighty Conn, and here's what he told me about what was coming next. *Zip. Nada. Nix. A big fat absolute nothing.* I don't think he was trying to be cute with the Geist-meister, but he just wouldn't talk. Maybe it was another new mysterioso move. But he wouldn't tell me one single thing about the new direction in which his musico-maniacal mind was motorvating.

"Still, it's got to be going somewhere. There was some serious energy-discharge at the Prinz Lorenz. The kind of fuel he was burning at the last show has put him straight into the stratosphere. So keep your eyes to the skies, girls and guys. It won't be long before you see a glow up there in the nighttime heavens, and it'll get brighter and hotter, and you'll hear a faraway wailing. And what goes up, as we all well know, must come down."

ABOUT THE AUTHOR

An avid musician, Leander Watts has played and sung for decades in a wide variety of bands. His interests range from garage rock to skronky jazz, from baroque organ to Appalachian gospel. The first rock concert he attended was David Bowie on the Diamond Dogs tour in 1974. He teaches writing and literature at the State University of New York at Geneseo (his alma mater). Leander Watts is the author of *Stonecutter*, *Wild Ride to Heaven*, *Ten Thousand Charms*, and *Beautiful City of the Dead*.